First paperback edition April 2023

The Ragged Man

On Nothing Hangs the Earth, Book 2

By Tom Kline

The Events of *On Nothing Hangs the Earth, Book 1*

The US has been attacked by a weaponized disease and its cities have fallen. David Gath and the crew of the International Space Station have returned to Earth with a vaccine to save what remains. After losing most of their team to mercenaries and the infected that roam the land, they arrive at an underground research facility to be told their mission is a lie. Gath and a handful of survivors escape into the frozen ruins of Washington DC.

On Nothing Hangs the Earth Book 2, The Ragged Man, begins on the morning of the final events of Book 1.

Prologue

But we are all like an unclean thing,
And all our righteousnesses are like filthy rags;
We all fade as a leaf,
And our iniquities, like the wind,
Have taken us away.
And there is no one who calls on Your name,
Who stirs himself up to take hold of You;
For You have hidden Your face from us,
And have consumed us because of our iniquities.

Isaiah 64: 6-7 New King James Bible

Chapter 1

The streets were silent under weeks of snow as darkness gave way to dawn. Wind raked across everywhere the used-to-be used to go. Then something stirred. It was big, 30 feet from nose to tail, and taller than a man. The scales were white, the eyes black and unblinking, facing forward like a predator. It lumbered through drifts and over debris as it made its way along the remnants of a road. There was a clank as it clipped an abandoned car, the sound of metal against metal exposing the creature for what it was. A machine, a man-made monster. The eyes bullet-proof windows, the scales armor composite. Its body was 20 tons of military-grade steel, painted to match the winter all around it. An artificial terror, but no less terrible for that.

The Oshkosh M-ATV was designed to protect US troops in Afghanistan. This one had been adapted to arctic warfare and converted to electricity to keep sound to a minimum. There were no mines or rocket attacks to worry about anymore, but noise could be just as deadly. It attracted the kind of attention even an M-ATV would rather avoid. A long barrel slid from the turret on top and tracked from side to side. Detecting movement, it swung to the left to find old canvas flapping in the wind. With no immediate threat, the gun rotated back to the center and retracted. Inside the armored vehicle was a sanctuary from the streets, but you couldn't hide forever. The city was quiet, the only sound the crunch of snow as the M-ATV rolled past wrecked cars and looted stores.

There were six people in the belly of the beast, strapped to their seats in snow camouflage. No one spoke as the vehicle crawled along, each thinking their own thoughts. Three were soldiers, two in the front and one facing the rear. Military Police, uniforms hidden under heavy parkas. Only combat webbing set them apart from the others. The soldier facing backward had his chin on his chest. Every time they hit a bump, his head bobbled, but he didn't wake up. Three scientists sat in the rear in jump seats. Dubchek was old and overweight, the parka unzipped to show a pink bow tie over a bulging stomach. He sat opposite two women. Prashad was young, her tan matching the color of her ponytail. She had that preppy look, like an overachiever. Lang was a black woman in her 40s, her face a perpetual frown.

No one wanted to be there. An early morning trip into a dead city wasn't anyone's idea of fun. They came from Aegis Laboratories; a Department of Defense bunker a thousand feet below ground. The soldiers hated the scientists, and the scientists hated each other. It wasn't a happy place. There was no small talk on their journey, no banter. That was fine with Lang, she wasn't there to make friends. They were living on borrowed time. Before the outbreak, Aegis had been geared toward weapons technology. The Director, Morton Bell, knew Congress loved weapons. They were the programs that got the most funding because they supported the troops, stirred patriotic pride, and poured billions of tax-payer dollars into corporations that donated prodigiously to both political parties.

After the outbreak, everything changed. Development Command ordered all installations to stop what they were doing and focus everything on the search for a vaccine. Bell, however, didn't think the end of the world was any reason for Aegis Laboratories to stop making weapons. Instead of joining the search for a cure, he doubled down on ways to kill the infected. When they lost contact with Greensboro and Evansville, their most advanced vaccine labs, Bell still prioritized ways to win a unique kind of war. A vaccine wouldn't help those who already had White's Disease. It wouldn't stop millions of infected swarming the survivors. Aegis Laboratories would continue to focus on keeping people alive in this new world that nobody wanted.

The vehicle lurched and everyone gripped the safety rail. They climbed up a steep bank of snow, thumping down on the other side. Corporal Mapuya was jolted awake and wiped the drool from his face. The M-ATV had to go slowly out of necessity, given the terrain and the need to keep noise to a minimum. This meant a 20-minute journey in days gone by now took a couple of hours. Prashad stretched.

"Is this your first time outside?"

"Yes," said Lang.

"You don't go when they collect specimens?"

"No."

"You should try heading out more often, that's the way to get the best results. I've been out twice getting samples. I like to select the tissue myself."

Lang ignored her. The girl was allowed outside to get samples because she was nobody. It didn't matter if she died. Lang, on the other hand, mattered a great deal. Before the outbreak, she created pathogens to incapacitate the enemy. Not to kill, which was banned by the UN Biological Weapons Convention, but to render fighting men ineffective. Helpless soldiers required the enemy to spend more resources caring for the injured and sapped morale. Now, her job was harder. She had been tasked with finding a way to target victims of White's Disease without harming uninfected humans. If they could create a way to wipe out the infected, they wouldn't have to live underground.

Director Bell expected results but so far, they had failed. They needed a game-changer, something to give a radical new approach to their research. So Lang proposed Operation Headhunter. The plan was simple. Send a team to Georgetown University to retrieve vital data left behind when the campus had been lost. Washington hadn't been evacuated. Admitting defeat was too hard for politicians and there was nowhere else to go. Some of the finest minds in cytopathology and molecular diagnostics had worked at Georgetown right to the end, airlifted out minutes before the campus had been overrun.

They died anyway, but their research survived, stored on computers at Georgetown. Lang had access to the campus and knew where to look. She made it clear that this data could mean the breakthrough they were looking for. The plan was dangerous, going into the city was always dangerous, but Bell gave the green light immediately. The fact that Lang knew the research would lead nowhere didn't bother her in the slightest. She had her own reasons to get to Georgetown.

"Where first?" asked Prashad. "Offices or labs?"

"You can start at Cole's office, I'll take Calderone's. We can meet up at the labs."

"We're supposed to stay together."

"We'll cover more ground if we split up."

"That won't work for us."

Lang scowled. "Won't work for you?"

"No. We'll do the offices, then the labs. Together."

Lang ground her teeth. Bringing other scientists had never been part of the plan. They were supposed to land a helicopter on the roof of the University Hospital, access the Medical Dental Building, locate the research, then return. All over in 30 minutes. Then the military stepped in, and everything changed. Going in by air was too risky, they said. A Super Huey made too much noise when it landed, the infected would swamp the helicopter. The operation had been changed to a ground insertion. Rival Divisions started interfering, trying to get some of the glory. When Human Research and Engineering proposed sending two of their scientists, Lang had refused, but it did her no good. Politics was a dirty game and Operation Headhunter wasn't her baby anymore.

Dubchek leaned forward and patted her knee.

"Best stick together, Jennifer. Besides, safety in numbers. I'm a bit nervous."

She produced a fake smile. "Don't be, Stan, it's perfectly safe. The drone said the place is locked up tight. Nothing to worry about."

"I don't have the cardio to run from the things, you see." He smiled in apology. "Too much KFC."

Lang shifted to look out of the window. The city was a white blur through the glass, but it was better entertainment than looking at Dubchek. A drone had mapped out the route and checked it again an hour before they left Aegis. This was the optimal route, but it was still taking too long. She felt the walls of the M-ATV closing in on her. It was warm and safe, but she needed to get out there, to find what she was looking for. The passengers swayed in their seats as they rolled over something big.

"Where are we?" she called to the front.

"North-West 37th Street," said Sergeant Copeland. "10 minutes out."

He was old for a soldier, with a gray buzzcut and a tired face. Lang nodded and closed her eyes, hoping that if she looked asleep no one would bother her. Time passed and she tried to relax.

"Dr. Lang?"

Her eyes opened. It was Copeland.

"A problem," he said. "Can't drive right up to the doors. Matvee won't fit."

A Matvee was what soldiers called the M-ATV.

"Why not?"

"Some kind of blockage. No way around."

"The drone said the route was clear."

"The drone was wrong."

"What's the closest we can get?"

"Reservoir Road. Looks like we can access the building from there."

A few more minutes and they finally came to a halt. Lang stood and grabbed her equipment. There wasn't enough room inside to stand straight. Dubchek and Prashad were on their feet, bent over, fussing like old women on a plane. Corporal Mapuya moved to the rear and helped them unload the gray plastic carry cases, one for each of the science staff.

"Clip your holster onto your utility belt," said the Corporal. "Make sure it's secure as instructed. The Sig P320 is perfectly safe unless you pull the trigger. Extra ammunition is in your right belt pouch."

The scientists all had pistols, but the soldiers had compact submachine guns. They had been briefed on the Brugger & Thomet APC9K. The little automatic weapon could kill before you could think. Sound was the surest way to draw the infected, so all weapons on Operation Headhunter had suppressors to reduce noise. Prashad had the pistol on her belt already, signifying her veteran status.

"In the unlikely event that you'll have to use your weapons," Mapuya continued, "please remember there are 12 rounds per magazine, and you have three mags. One already seated, two in the pouch. Check your spares now."

Dubchek was having trouble putting on his holster and Mapuya strapped it on for him.

"All ammunition is Polymer Kinetic Ejection. Hit center mass and they will explode and drop the target."

"Won't that be loud?" asked Dubchek.

"PIKE rounds are frangible, they break into fragments shredding the target. There's no boom." He smiled. "Your face covering and eye protection go on like this."

The soldier demonstrated by putting on his own headgear. "It's well below freezing outside, so don't take off your face covering or goggles." He put on his helmet.

Lang fitted her headgear and cinched the parka's hood in place. Though the scientists worked for the Department of Defense, they were civilians. Dressing up in camouflage gear and strapping on guns was new to them and Lang felt the unfamiliar tingle of excitement. The scientists picked up their cases.

"Ready?" asked Mapuya.

He didn't wait for a reply. The Corporal opened one of the rear hatches, dropping it to make a ramp to the hip-deep snow. They could hear the wind now as the temperature dropped. Their parkas, pants, and gloves were coated with silver nanowire mesh that heated their camouflage gear, so they would be warm as long as the batteries lasted. Lang negotiated her way down the ramp. Reservoir Road was unrecognizable. There were no cars or ruins, only frozen trees marred the uniform white of the boulevard.

"We're going up those steps," said Lang.

Copeland nodded. "You first."

"I thought soldiers go first?"

"You know the way," he tapped the screen on the back of his weapon. "I'm right behind you with the Merson."

The Merson was an experimental gadget from Aegis, an echolocator that used sound waves to detect movement. The team had Friend or Foe chips in their arms that showed up as their initial in blue. Any other movement was a red dot. Lang took a deep breath. The fabric of the mask made the cold air bearable. Mapuya took the rear, helping Dubchek who was already having difficulty. Prashad was in the middle. Corporal Erlich would wait with the vehicle and provide covering fire if they had to fall back.

Pillars flanked the steps up the middle of the grass verge. *School of Dentistry* was on the left-hand side, *School of Medicine* on the right. Lang's footing was sure in the big Belleville military boots they made her wear. At the top was a road whited out by snow. The grand façade of the Medical Dental Building sat opposite. It was huge, over a hundred yards in each direction, four stories high with tall columns and wrought iron railings. Five sets of glass and walnut double doors ran along the front. Lang chose the center door and wiped frost from the security panel. Pulling off a glove, she pressed her thumb down. The lock clicked and the door opened, just as if the world hadn't ended.

Lang pushed in and swept the curtain aside. The smell brought back memories. Old wood and floor polish. It was dark inside, but she moved forward anyway to let the others into the lobby. There was enough light to see until someone closed the doors. It was pitch black, then weapon lights snapped on. The lobby was spacious with a high ceiling and mementos decorating the paneled walls. There were two closed doors and a hallway stretching away. Lang clicked on her flashlight and shone it around the room, remembering the first time she had walked on the parquet floor. Dubchek sniffed the air a few times, then coughed.

"Is it OK if I take the mask off? I have allergies."

With no objections, he set down his case and stripped off his headgear. He took a few loud breaths and smiled broadly. Lang and Prashad exchanged looks and did the same.

"Sound carries inside," said Copeland. "Remember noise discipline."

"What do you mean?" asked Dubchek.

"Keep talk to a minimum."

The old scientist chuckled. "I love to talk, Sergeant. Maybe I should go back to the transport."

"Fine by me, Doctor."

Lang started walking down the hallway and Copeland caught up with her.

"Wait for the others, Dr. Lang."

"Why? It's safe."

"We don't know that."

The party moved deeper into the building, Prashad and Dubchek bringing up the rear. The Medical Dental Building was famous for being a warren at the best of times. It didn't take long before only Lang knew where they were.

Dubchek couldn't cope with the pace, but she didn't slow down. The man was a liability. They passed a sign saying *Department of Microbiology and Immunology*, went through a small reception area, and into another hallway. Dubchek was wheezing now. Lang stopped at a door with an inset window. To the side was a nameplate. *Professor Michael Cole*. She tried the handle, but it was locked.

"I'll check the neighborhood," said Copeland.

He walked off into the blackness. Left alone with Prashad and Dubchek, Lang was at a loss. She knew her way around a lab and that was about it. Deciding she needed more information, she examined the window in the door with her flashlight.

"Right. Take out your first aid kits."

The other scientists did as they were told.

"Give me the big square sticking plasters. Both of them."

"Why?" asked Prashad.

"Just do it."

Prashad and Dubchek, out of their depth, handed over the plasters.

"Aim your lights at the glass."

Lang stripped the backing and stuck the adhesive side to the window in the door. With the two from her own kit, she had a beige rectangle covering the center of the glass panel. She unclipped her hip holster and drew the pistol.

"What are you doing?" asked Prashad.

Lang aimed and fired. Even with the suppressor, it was loud. Like a nail gun. The frangible PIKE round hit the center of the sticking plasters and broke apart, punching a fist-sized hole in the glass. Copeland came running back.

"What the fuck are you doing?"

He was angry but he kept his voice low.

"Getting into the office," said Lang.

She walked to the window and pushed her gloved hand through. A section of the glass fell out, landing on the floor with a clack. The adhesive kept the shattered pieces together and there was no sound of smashing.

Copeland was in her face. "I told you we needed noise discipline."

"That was as disciplined as I could make it."

Lang opened the door with a flourish. The Sergeant took a step toward her, standing too close.

"You should listen to me, Doctor. I'm the only thing stopping you from being someone's lunch."

Chapter 2

Mambo Mango - Take a Tempting, Tantalizing Taste Today. The poster was at the center of a brightly colored display that dominated the produce section. Boxes were stacked in a pyramid under the picture of a woman in a bikini holding the fruit. She looked like she wanted nothing more than to sink her teeth into something succulent, to feel the juice running down her chin. It was a great advertisement, making you think of food and sex at the same time. Always a winner. The sales pitch, however, did not measure up to reality. In real life, the fruit didn't tempt, didn't tantalize, and was the last thing you'd want to sink your teeth into. A sickly smell came from the rows of blackened husks below the picture. The decayed remains were now a different kind of advertisement, one that bore witness to this new world. In that, the rotten fruit measured up to reality perfectly.

Gloria lifted a red scarf over her nose as she stared at the remains around her. When the end came, this branch of Safeway had been left untouched. The shelves of the place were filled with canned and boxed goods of every kind, enough to feed a family for years. Fresh food had not fared so well, and the smell of decay was everywhere. She looked at the remains and was startled by the rush of emotion. What a waste. Right then, Gloria wanted nothing more than a fresh mango. Filled with a need she couldn't explain, her mouth began to water. But it was impossible. She would never eat a fresh mango again. Despair touched her and tears began. What was happening to her? She hadn't cried when disease swept the city or when her friends died. But now she looked at ranks of rotten fruit and began to weep uncontrollably. Angry, she rubbed at her eyes, shaking, and looked away. She didn't even like fucking mangos.

Gloria Bruno knew she was an attractive woman. Not one of those half-starved waifs on the cover of Vogue, but a real woman. Tall and strong with plenty of curves. At 42 she easily passed for someone ten years younger. Not that she admitted to 42, as if aging was something to feel guilty about. Gloria was always dressed in red; disaster didn't change that. She wore a scarlet Everest windbreaker and matching Ulla Popken ski pants. Her boots were brown, which was annoying, but they were warm and waterproof and would do until she found red ones. There was nobody around to look at her anyway. Nobody that mattered.

"Glory!"

She hated being called that. Gloria wiped her eyes but didn't reply. An older man emerged from Household Essentials. Short and fat, he wore an orange Arctic survival jacket with a full-faced respirator pushed back on his head. Across his back was an emergency axe and he had a compact crossbow holstered at his hip. The weapons seemed out of place.

"Shouldn't wander off."

"There's no one here, Howard."

Howard seemed to process this for a while, then his face broke into a lopsided grin. All his grins were lopsided.

"I got you a surprise."

"What is it?"

"If I said, it wouldn't be a surprise."

She didn't argue and walked away from the produce section. It annoyed Gloria when Howard wouldn't answer her questions, but he annoyed her anyway. She tried to think of a time when Howard wasn't annoying but couldn't. Gloria moved to the doors where four large olive green backpacks sat taped to a surfboard. The board had ropes nailed to it so they could pull the thing across the snow. It wasn't perfect and packs occasionally fell off, but it was a hell of a lot better than carrying the stuff on their backs. There was a small burgundy bag on top. That was hers, a few essentials cherrypicked from all the crap. Howard hobbled around the corner with a last-minute armful of supplies and started wedging them into one of the backpacks. Gloria watched him with her arms crossed. Howard pulled down the respirator. It was transparent and he was still grinning.

"Home again, home again, jiggety-jig!"

He lifted his hood and opened the front doors. Wind hit them as they grabbed the ropes and dragged the surfboard out into the freezing cold. They made good progress over the uneven terrain, though each step through snow this deep was an effort. It was a short trip down the street, hardly qualifying as a stroll in ordinary times. But now it would take them 20 minutes to get the board back with all the bags. It was a routine trip now. The first time they had gone, Gloria was terrified. But there was nothing. No infected, no bodies. Not above the ice, anyway.

They weren't starving, Howard had enough food for months, but it was all things he liked. Fried breakfasts and instant burritos were all very well, but Gloria wanted more. She hunted little luxuries while Howard stocked up for the long haul. He was struggling now as they dragged the board, but this was nothing new. Before they had found the snowboard in a store display and pressed it into service, Howard would turn purple with a pack on his back. His breathing came in fits and starts but Gloria didn't stop. He needed the exercise.

Howard finally dropped the rope when they reached No. 1726, putting his hands on his hips to help get air into his lungs. Gloria stared at the cream and brick storefront. *First Cash, Jewelry & Loan*. Howard's apartment was upstairs, but this wasn't where they lived. His breath back, Howard picked up the rope and they started moving again. 30 yards farther was a gate in a low wall that ran between No. 1726 and the realtor next door. They dragged the surfboard through into the private car lot behind the buildings. There, out of sight of the road, was their real home.

Her name was Dorothy, a UNICAT Expedition Ultimate Recreational Vehicle. A 30-foot-long truck connected to a trailer of the same length by an articulated sleeve. She was 40 tons of beige and chrome with a blast-proof chassis, Runflat tires, and Armorglass windows. She had solar panels, a recycling system, reinforced doors, and an onboard computer. Dorothy had kept them safe as the city died.

"Honey, I'm home!" called Howard.

Dorothy opened the shutters in the rear trailer, as she had been programmed. Howard lifted the backpacks and carried them up the ramp into the storage area.

Howard Hankey had been a bookkeeper for an insurance company in Mount Pleasant. An undistinguished arts graduate of McDaniel College, he took a temporary job with the small family firm to stop his mother from nagging. He stayed there for 35 years. It was a sleepy, uninspiring place, run badly for little profit. Howard was their bookkeeper because he knew how to add, and they didn't want to pay an accountant. His mother died the day Obama was elected, killed by Camels and conservative views. Howard borrowed the money to bury her. Apart from an alcoholic aunt in Vegas, he was the only Hankey left. He lived a quiet life, unafflicted by anything of interest to anyone.

Until the aunt died and left him eight million dollars. Dorothy Hankey was an expert at drinking rum and playing blackjack, investing her winnings in stocks and real estate. Howard's life changed forever. He quit his job and bought the little apartment he rented above a pawnshop on Wisconsin Avenue. For him, the good life didn't mean the golf club or exotic vacations, no hookers or cocaine. He decided to be what he always wanted to be. A prepper. Howard had always been awed by those men on TV who were prepared for anything, who converted cabins into castles or basements into bunkers. They would still be standing when the world was dust.

Howard knew he was a loser, but that didn't mean he couldn't dream. He fantasized about having his own place, self-contained and self-reliant, safe and protected. It gave him a contentment he never thought possible. Every day someone was predicting Armageddon. Nobody knew if the end was nigh, but if it was, Howard wanted to be prepared. In the quiet moments tucked up in bed, Howard indulged in his guilty fantasy. Howard Hankey, Last Man on Earth! With his aunt's passing, he had the means to make his dream come true. He bought an End of the World RV and named it after the woman who had made it all possible. Dorothy became his obsession.

Howard's other obsession was food. He didn't have a fine palate, but he could afford to go to the best restaurants, so he did. Dining at the finest eateries in Washington and tipping lavishly, he became a fixture at Xiquet, Marcel's, and The Lafayette. He met Gloria for the first time when he decided to try a fusion hipster restaurant in Columbia Heights. Gloria was 38 and newly divorced when she took over as manager of the Rooster & Owl. She needed a fresh start and this was a golden opportunity. Gloria met Howard at the door in her second week on the job. She beamed at him and, for the first time in his life, Howard fell in love.

Gloria didn't think much of the fat little man but insulting the customers was never a recipe for success. She fussed over him, helped him choose the right dishes, and made him feel like a king. From that day on, he was hooked.

The way he looked at her was annoying, but he praised the food and tipped like an Arab, so he was always welcome. Howard called her Glory right from the start, mishearing her name. He kept it up, believing it gave him a special place in her affections. It didn't. She swallowed the irritation every time he said it and let him plop into his seat, unadmonished, ready for filet mignon and fries. He kept on overpaying and she took his money with a smile.

Then the world ended. It was just a normal December evening until everyone stopped what they were doing and stared at their phones. To Gloria, phones during dinner were the devil. She frowned on distractions. No TV, no cabaret, no loud music. The Rooster offered a muted, intimate experience for the discerning customer. In her old job, she put up one of those notices. *No, we don't have wifi, talk to each other*, but now everyone had 5G. Gloria had to innovate and use candles, music, and incense to get people to concentrate on food and conversation. But this was something different, something big. She could feel it, rippling around the room.

"Fuck me," said Miguel, a waiter, breaking her No Cursing rule. "They blew up Detrick."

Fort Detrick was a major army base an hour's drive north. The bombing was the only story on the news shows, diplomatic ties with Russia were cut, and all anyone could talk about was war. Then people started getting sick. It was a rumor at first, then stuff online. Nobody knew what to believe. Washington was a government town and she had lots of regulars who worked on the Hill. They said nothing but they all looked worried. Someone posted a video on Youtube of a woman eating a hand. It was like a bad movie but it was real and you couldn't turn it off. People stayed at home and locked their doors. Only a handful of customers still came to the Rooster, older people who didn't watch TV or didn't care. And Howard, always Howard, sitting at the same table at the same time every night, ordering the same thing, smiling his bent smile.

Quarantines were imposed and there was a media blackout in Maryland and Virginia. The nightly news was one long list of the terrible. Christmas saw record-low numbers in stores and record-high numbers in church. The Rooster was losing money hand over fist, but no one cared about profits anymore. Just when Gloria thought it couldn't get any worse, it got worse. Live shows stopped and the internet went offline. FEMA, the Federal Emergency Management Agency, ran announcements 24/7 with occasional briefings from the White House Press Secretary.

Supermarkets ran out of fresh food, fights broke out, then they were closed by the army. FEMA started giving out supplies, boxes of emergency rations, and bottled water from the back of trucks. Coming up to New Year, the Rooster stopped taking money and making menus. Ronny cooked up whatever was left in the kitchen for staff and anyone else who happened by. It looked like New Year's Eve was going to be canceled until a big blue Suburban turned up one morning. Men carried in bags of food, eggs, bread, meat; stuff you couldn't buy anymore. Howard had saved the day.

December 31st was the last night for the Rooster & Owl. Customers and staff ate a feast together and toasted the New Year with the last of the liquor. For one night they tried to forget their days were numbered, and that number was low. As people left in heavy coats to ward off the cold, too drunk to drive but driving anyway, Howard walked Gloria to her car.

"If things get worse, I have a place," he said, mumbling like a boy at the prom. "It's safe, it has everything. You could stay there. As a friend, I mean. If things go bad, there's a place. I just wanted you to know."

Gloria didn't know what to say so she said nothing. Howard's head bobbed.

"You can call me. Here's my number. Call if you need me."

He held out an old-fashioned printed card with a phone number but no name. Gloria stared at him. This was awkward and she wanted to get away. She took the card, said something she couldn't remember, and got into her convertible. Stuffing the card into her pocket she drove away, not looking back. Her eighth-floor apartment in Edgewood was waiting, all stocked up. Everything she and Barney would need for the next couple of weeks. The Ginger Tom was picky, but she had his favorite, Made by Nacho. Cuts in Gravy. He would eat better than she would tonight. Things would be fine in a few weeks, she knew they would. They would hole up, get fat, and ride out the storm.

It was after 2 am when she got home. Barney was on the apartment steps, waiting for her. His head was gone, blood matting most of the fur on his little body. Down the block, someone was yelling. Gloria hurried inside, leaving Barney where he lay, and pressed the elevator button. Nothing happened. She hit it again. Panic threatened to overwhelm her as she ran to the stairwell. The eight flights up were terrifying. Lights were out and she had to use her phone to see. Let the power in her place still be on! By the time she put the key in the lock, she was finding it hard to breathe.

Gloria slammed the door closed and threw the bolts. Relief flooded through her. She was home, safe. When she calmed down enough to move, she walked to the kitchen and turned on the kettle. Opening the cupboard, she grabbed some instant and spooned it into a mug. Adding water, she drank it too quickly and scalded her tongue. Her hands were shaking. Who would do that to a cat? Gloria closed the curtains, switched on the lamp, and took down a bottle of Johnnie Walker. Pouring way too much into her coffee, she added a little more and lay down on the couch.

Feeling for the remote, she clicked on the TV. The President was taking questions, but the sound was off. He looked very old. A scrolling caption at the bottom of the screen said *President Evacuates to White House Bunker. Public Urged Not to Panic.* Gloria read the words again. This couldn't be happening. Shivering, she got up to warm milk for the cat, then she remembered Barney didn't need milk anymore. A car alarm started in the street below. Gloria sat down again and searched her pockets for the card. She tried not to cry as she typed Howard's number into her phone.

Chapter 3

Lang watched with contempt as they broke into filing cabinets and rifled through drawers. Bottom-feeding scum. She used to work with Mike Cole, if anyone had the right to take his research, it was her. Lang had never liked the man, but that wasn't the point. These two were scavengers, not fit to lick a real scientist's boots. Prashad sat down and started the desk computer, connecting a slim portable drive. It was a Ripper, another Aegis device. It bypassed security protocols and harvested material from the computer's memory.

"Which part of Mike's work are you looking for?" asked Lang.

Prashad lifted her eyes from the screen. "Interactions of the mucosal immune system with the commensal microbiota of the oropharynx."

"Why?"

Prashad looked at Dubchek.

"We can't really discuss it, Jennifer," said the old man, smiling. "You know how it is."

"It's fine, Stan. We're old hands, we know the score. I was just trying to help. Mike and I were close."

Prashad stood up. "We can't find his sample data. Do you know where it is?"

"No," said Lang, smiling.

Prashad scowled. The Ripper had completed its task so the woman removed it and went to help Dubchek with the cabinets. Lang left the office. The corridor outside was empty. She walked until she saw Copeland's weapon light around the corner. He was staring at antique medical devices laid out on the shelves and didn't notice her. Not very soldierly.

"René Laennec Stethoscope," said Lang, reading over his shoulder, causing him to turn. "Necker–Enfants Malades Hospital, 1816."

"Don't creep around."

"I thought you wanted noise discipline?"

Copeland cursed and walked passed her, back to the office. Lang followed and they stopped outside, waiting for the others to finish.

"Interested in medicine?" asked Lang.

"No."

"What were you reading?"

"I was thinking."

"About what?"

Copeland shrugged. "The past."

"You're a history buff?"

"I was thinking. I'm allowed to think."

Dubchek and Prashad came out, tucking the last of their finds into the carry cases.

"Calderone's office now," said Prashad.

Lang led the way along the corridor and off to the right. Prashad was annoying her. Not because she was rude, but because she didn't seem to be afraid. Lang was Head of the Biological Agents Section of the Weapons and Materials Research Division. She briefed Congress and the White House. Prashad was a junior researcher at Overmatch Solutions. Lang could squash her like a bug. Dubchek was her Section Head, but that old oxygen thief couldn't help her. He was a joke, only in the job because all the better men were dead. Compared to Overmatch Solutions, being dead was a step up.

Lang led them along another corridor, through an open-plan meeting area, then on to a laboratory complex. There was a row of labs on either side of the passageway, each with a sliding door and a fingerprint lock. Lang walked to the nearest and pressed a thumb on the security panel. It glowed green and the door slid open.

"These labs have everything you need. The door will open automatically until I lock it again."

"These labs?" asked Prashad. "Are there more?"

"This is Georgetown, there are hundreds of labs. Stan, what equipment do you need?"

The old man hesitated and Prashad rattled it off.

"A centrifuge, autosamplers, dispensing tools, and microhomogenizers."

"They're all in here."

"What if we need something else?"

"You won't."

"But what if we do?"

"Then you're shit out of luck."

Dubchek raised a placating hand. "These labs will be fine, Jennifer. We can come back after we search Professor Calderone's office."

"I want to look in the other labs too," said Prashad. "Who knows what we'll find."

"This isn't a mall."

"You don't own the place."

Lang jabbed a finger at the woman. "Why don't you fuck off back to whatever shithole you came from."

"Stanford."

"Then fuck off back to Stanford, you pissy little bitch. I have access to Georgetown because the Dean respects me, not because I suck fratboy cock."

Prashad smiled. "Since the Dean's dead or out there shitting himself and eating dogs, it hardly matters. Where's Calderone's office?"

Copeland was enjoying the show but Dubchek looked like he wanted to go back to bed. Lang would have loved to kick the younger woman's head in, but she walked away and the lab door closed. She had bigger fish to fry. As they went to the next office, Dubchek tried to change the subject.

"Did you work in this department, Jennifer?"

"No, Biochemistry."

"You know your way around."

"We ran joint projects."

The long walk was making Dubchek sweat. "Where was your office?"

"I didn't have one. I was a Visiting Professor, on campus once a week. I worked out of the Faculty Office."

Lang stopped. Her flashlight pointed at a sturdy wooden door with *Professor R. Calderone, Department Chair* printed on it. There was no glass in the door this time. Lang tried the handle and the door opened. Copeland moved past her to check the office was clear. It was big, three times the size of Cole's, with a coffee table, desk, two armchairs, and a couch beside a well-stocked bookcase.

"Are we going to take two copies of everything or share?" asked Lang.

Prashad and Dubchek exchanged looks and the older man nodded. "As soon as we get back, I'll have copies made."

He was lying, but at least he had the decency to look uncomfortable. Divisions at Aegis didn't share. Lang knew this as well as anyone. She had only asked to make Dubchek squirm. Within minutes, there were mounds of documents stacked on the coffee table. They were getting good at stealing other people's work. Dubchek assembled a tower of hardback books. The older man gave her a sheepish grin.

"I miss real books."

"You should take more. They're limited editions."

"Are they?"

"All books are limited editions now, Stan."

Lang took her gloves off and made a show of assembling some of the more important files for about twenty minutes, to look convincing, then brushed the dust off her hands.

"I'm going to the washroom. You guys finish up."

"We're supposed to stay together," said Prashad.

"I don't think that includes taking a shit."

Prashad was going to argue but Dubchek nodded. "Of course, Jennifer. We can finish off here then all go back to the labs."

Lang put her gloves back on and walked into the hallway. Copeland was leaning against a wall, eyes on the Merson. He trusted the device too much.

"I'm going to go to the washroom."

The man looked up. "I have to come with you."

"You're kidding."

"Orders."

"Is that what you call it?"

"There may be infected."

"The building's empty."

"I have my orders."

"Aren't you supposed to be on guard? What if someone slits Dr. Prashad's throat while you're checking me out in the stalls?"

Copeland was uncertain. "How far is it?"

"Five minutes."

"Let's go and look."

When they arrived at the washroom, Lang hung back while the Sergeant nudged the door open.

"Wait here," he said.

He went inside, then came out.

"Clear."

"Of course it's clear."

"I'll stay here. I won't go in."

"I'm not having you out here listening to my bowel movements."

"The building's not secure."

Lang stood close to him. "Are you in love with me, Sergeant?"

"What?"

"It's a simple question. Are you in love with me?"

"You're crazy."

"So you just want sex, is that it? Something quick? Something dirty?"

"Stop fucking around."

Lang leaned forward, forcing him to take a step back.

"We can do it now if you want. I won't tell anyone. But I like it rough, Sergeant. Very rough."

Copeland frowned. "If you're not back in 20, I'm knocking on the stall door."

He walked away. Lang waited for his weapon light to disappear around a corner, then headed quickly in the opposite direction. 20 minutes. Not much time, but it would be enough. Lang walked as quickly as she could for the first minute, the flashlight sweeping out ahead, then she broke into a run. After five minutes, she slowed to take the stairs. Walking for a while to get her breath back, she started jogging. There it was. *Department of Biochemistry and Molecular & Cellular Biology*. It didn't take long to find the double doors marked *Faculty Office*. She put a thumb on the security panel and there was a click. Shining her light inside, cold air touched her face.

The window at the back of the big office was smashed. Snow piled on the carpet tiles around it. The place was a mess, but the lockers lined along one side were untouched. Lang walked across the room, banging into a table and cursing. At the lockers, she took off a glove and typed in the code. Nothing happened. Blowing warm air onto her fingers, she tried again. The door popped open. Inside was only one item, a thick pink notebook. She put her glove back on and lifted the book out, touching her forehead to the cover. This was it. This was the real game-changer.

"Hello, Jennifer."

Lang froze. The voice was so unexpected, she wondered if she had imagined it. Dubchek was standing in the doorway, flashlight in hand, like an old movie villain. Neither said a word. Wind whistled through the broken window.

"I thought we'd lost you," said Dubchek.

"Just picking something up." Lang squinted in the light. "Personal stuff."

"I think we both know that's not true."

"Are you calling me a liar, Stan?"

"I'm afraid I am, Jennifer." Dubchek walked towards her. "When the Sergeant came back without you, I knew you'd be in your old department. They told me you were looking for something. Something important."

He stopped a few feet away.

"Who told you?" asked Lang.

Dubchek smiled and reached out a hand. "May I?"

Lang had misjudged the fat man. He was cleverer than he looked. With no option, she handed him the notebook.

"Thank you for not making a fuss, Jennifer."

The older man held up his flashlight and flicked through the pages.

"You're a talented woman, Jennifer, I've always admired that. But other people have talent too. The Sergeant will be here soon, then we can go home."

Dubchek stopped at a page and read more intently. His expression of mild interest turned to one of surprise and he looked up.

The bullet struck him in the chest.

After the crack of the shot, there was no sound. The man clawed at the hole in his parka as a patch of red appeared around it. Dubchek tried to say something, but the PIKE round had done its job. He coughed up blood and collapsed, the notebook skidding across the floor. Lang's flashlight lingered on the body. She had never killed anyone before. Not directly. There wasn't much time. She ran to the doors, slammed them shut, and pressed her thumb to the lock. Recovering the book, she zipped it into her inside pocket. A fist hammered from outside.

Moving to the window, Lang used her pistol barrel to break out more of the glass. Someone was kicking the doors now, but she ignored it and climbed over the window frame. In the freezing air, she found herself at the top of a small hill that sloped down to a footpath running east to west. Wind buffeted her as she started down the hill, slipping towards the end and sliding the rest of the way. She rolled across the pathway and ended up in a drift on the other side. Lying in a heap, she looked back up the hill.

Shouts came from inside the Faculty Office and she buried herself deep in the snow. It was thick where she lay, heaped around her like fresh linen. If she ran now, she would be a sitting duck, so she stayed where she was. Dressed in white and covered in snow, she would be hard to spot from the window. There was no way to avoid the Merson, but even if the gadget worked properly Copeland wouldn't be able to see her. He would have to come down the hill, which would give her a chance to run. There was a shout from the Faculty Office. It came again. He was calling her name.

Lang's face was going numb so she fished out the mask and goggles and put them back on. It wouldn't be long before Copeland figured out where she went. As she lay still, she saw movement to the east. People were spilling out of the Dahlgren Library, a few hundred yards away. There were dozens of them, milling about, movements jerky and erratic. Infected. Panic bloomed in the pit of her stomach and began to grow. There was another shout. Up the hill, she saw Copeland's helmet and heard her name. The infected heard it too and started running toward her along the footpath.

The Sergeant shouted again, waving his gun in her direction. It wouldn't be long before the infected were on her. She would have to surrender to Copeland or be eaten alive. Not much of a choice. Lang tried to think of a way out, but there wasn't one. She would have to scramble up the hill and climb back through the window. The infected were halfway to her. Lang could see the faces now. Shriveled and gnarled by the cold, the skin was gashed and torn. Their eyes were white and unblinking. It was the first time she had seen living infected. Hard to believe they were still alive.

Copeland kept on calling to her but he didn't shoot at the infected. Lang couldn't understand why until she realized he couldn't see them from where he was. He would have to stick his head out and look east, but he had no idea they were there. She was about to stand and run back up the hill when the Sergeant, fury overcoming him, screamed even louder. The infected changed direction, running up toward the Faculty Office. They strained and chuffed up the eastern slope of the hill, like dogs that couldn't bark. Nothing could be heard over the wind and Copeland wouldn't hear them until it was too late.

Lang stayed where she was and watched, fascinated. His only chance was the Merson, which was no chance at all. It was a pity. She had a sneaking admiration for the man. He was strong, decisive, and didn't take any shit. But he couldn't be allowed to make it back to Aegis and tell them what she had done. The infected reached the window and grabbed at Copeland, dragging him out. Lang couldn't see their teeth but saw the heads bury themselves into his back and neck. She got to her feet and headed west around the edge of the campus, back to the M-ATV.

Chapter 4

Gloria could smell the bacon frying before she opened her eyes. One of the things she least liked about aging, and it was up against some pretty stiff competition, was the amount of time it took to fully wake up. The time between opening your eyes and feeling really awake was what she called the Fog. Hating the Fog was the only part of this new life that was the same as the old. Gloria rolled out of bed, stretched, and ran a hand over her stomach. She needed to do more sit-ups. Being cooped up in here for weeks hadn't been easy, but there was enough self-awareness in her to realize she was lucky. Not many people were waking up to the smell of bacon. Not many were waking up at all.

Gloria slipped a rose-colored gown over her shoulders, pulling her long hair out of the collar. She looked at the mirror on the inside of her closet door. Still a fine-looking woman. How long would it last? She felt faintly guilty about obsessing over her looks, but only faintly. Though she was much more than the sum of her physical attributes, she had a terror of the day men stopped noticing her. The battle to stay desirable was always at the forefront of her mind, but one day she knew she would lose.

"Not today," she said out loud.

Unlatching the door, she stepped into the living room. The largest place inside Dorothy, the 20-by-12-foot space had a sofa, armchairs, and a TV as well as the kitchen. The top half of Howard's ridiculous green kimono was visible over the breakfast bar.

"I love the smell of napalm in the morning," he said, waving his spatula.

She had tried telling him that she wasn't interested in movie quotes, but people like Howard saw a lack of interest as an excuse to talk more. Gloria padded down the narrow gangway to the shower. She hung up her gown and turned on the water. Immediate warmth jetted out, cascading down her body. Were they getting hot showers in the FEMA camps? Were there camps anymore? She knew nothing of the world beyond Washington. Nothing of the world outside the street they lived on. There had been no refugee camps in DC, but she had heard rumors of places in Maryland and Virginia. Gloria used to daydream of rescue, of being sent to a modern, well-provisioned camp, and of being with other people. But weeks had passed and no one came.

Life now wasn't much, but she was still alive. In terms of food, drink, and hot running water, she lived better than many had in the time before. Compared to what lay outside, it was paradise. Her only problem was Howard. Under the steady stream of warm water, her muscles relaxed and her mind wandered to her favorite fantasy. She would be outside, getting provisions, when she was attacked by the infected. When all seemed lost, a man would appear. Of course, he was tall and handsome. He would fight his way to her side and they would run away, spending the night together, huddled for warmth. It would be entirely innocent. Innocence always excited her the most. She could smell his musk, and feel rock-hard muscles under his silky skin. He would protect her against anything. Her hero!

"Breakfast is done, hun bun!" called Howard.

Gloria's eyes narrowed. Howard was nobody's idea of a hero. A head shorter than her, fat, and mostly bald in a way that made you prefer bald, he didn't have any redeeming physical features. It was true there were men who were attractive despite their looks, men who had uncanny wisdom or were infectiously funny. Howard didn't have anything like that. It wasn't that he was a bad man, it was just that he wasn't much of a man at all. If she lined up every male customer who had ever eaten at the Rooster & Owl in order of desirability, Howard would be third from the bottom. The only men below him were Dirty Ken who smelled of piss and Dr. Ragano, who murdered his wife. Even Dr. Ragano might have been better. After all, he only killed one of his wives.

Drying herself with a fluffy towel, Gloria put on her gown and headed back out. She made a beeline for the breakfast bar. Howard was shoveling canned mushrooms from the pan onto a plate of bacon and scrambled eggs. She preferred sunny side up but there were no fresh eggs anymore. Gloria stabbed a mushroom and felt a speck of hot oil hit her knuckle. She licked it off. Howard sat opposite, staring at her as always. It had long since ceased to be annoying and was now just a fact of life, like piles. He poured coffee while she wolfed down the food.

"Soylent Green is people," said Howard, grinning.

Whatever. He had the hamster look right then, a hamster with a stupid grin. It was less irritating than the rat look. She wasn't sure what the difference was except she couldn't stand the rat look. This was mean and she knew it was mean, but as long as she didn't actually say anything, it wasn't cruel. Those were the rules. She had to share Dorothy with Howard, but her thoughts were her own. Howard brought out a thin lime-colored box and laid it in front of her.

"What's that?" she asked.

"Your surprise!"

Oh, right, the surprise. She had forgotten. Gloria kept on forking up the last of the egg. The box had *Miami Beach Chocolates* across the front, with the O in the middle designed as a little wave. Gloria loved chocolates, but she didn't react, it would only encourage Howard. Picking up the box, she set them on her lap and continued her breakfast. These babies weren't for sharing or eating one at a time. Gloria always found it best to eat gourmet chocolates all at once, then spend the rest of the week paying for the calories with guilt. If Howard was disappointed, he didn't show it. He smiled his hamster smile and chewed the toast. He lifted a waterproof map from the sideboard.

"I found a place. Arc'teryx," he continued. "Outdoors stuff, hiking, and ski gear. A guy from Arc'teryx told me where to buy my specialist stuff. Leon."

"The store guy told you to shop somewhere else. Must be a great place."

"It's fine for Main Street. Leon just wanted me to get the good stuff."

"Leon?"

"He made me a list."

"Was Leon doing this out of the goodness of his heart?"

"A nice guy."

"How much did you pay him?"

"He didn't do it for the money."

"How much?"

"A thousand."

Gloria sniffed. "Lucky Leon."

"I would've got more cold-weather stuff, but no one expected DC to get this bad. It freezes all the time, but not permafrost. This is not just new weather, it's a whole new climate."

"So much for global warming."

Gloria drank her coffee and Howard looked at his map. She normally didn't ask Howard questions to avoid an hour-long lecture on the birth of motion pictures or the best way to treat sewage, but she dipped in a toe.

"How did the climate change?"

He blinked. "Um…I don't know. Meteor, maybe. If a big enough meteor hits the Earth, dust, and stuff go into the air and everything goes dark."

"It's not dark, Howard."

"I'm just saying. Could be a nuclear attack. Atomic detonations can cause giant fires that send carbon into the atmosphere. Nuclear winter."

"There were no bombs."

"Well, we don't know that for sure," said Howard, warming to the topic. "It could happen hundreds of miles away. We're talking about explosions thousands of times more powerful than Hiroshima. DC wasn't hit, though, so I guess there was no nuclear war. We'd be the first on their list."

"Whose list?"

"Russia, China, anyone."

"Maybe they didn't attack because everyone's dead."

"Everyone but us," said Howard, smiling.

Gloria looked down at her plate. If it weren't for Howard, she would have died with everyone else, but gratitude came hard. She had never even thanked him. He had offered her sanctuary she was forced to accept and, though she was glad to be alive, she felt used. He hadn't laid a hand on her, hadn't asked for her body in exchange for her life, but he wasn't St. Francis of Assisi either. Howard didn't save her because he was a good person, he saved her because he thought he was in love. But great tits and love weren't the same thing.

"I made a list," he said. "It's three miles to the store. Maybe we won't bring the surfboard, travel light with our backpacks. If we find a lot of stuff, we can always make another trip."

"What if it's burned out?"

"Then we go to the Co-op. But that's over on Delaware, an extra two hours each way. It'd be night on the way back. We've never been out at night."

"Co-op might be burned out too."

Lots of buildings had caught fire when the end came, with looting and the army trying to stop the infected.

"We don't have to go if you don't want to," said Howard.

He didn't want to go, the trip was Gloria's idea. She needed to get out of Dorothy. As much as she loved the old girl, it came with Howard attached and for the sake of her sanity, she needed a change of scene. Besides, who knew what was out there? They might find survivors or soldiers, maybe even get rescued. Rescue was the last thing Howard wanted. Though he never said as much, she knew he was living the prepper wet dream. Bacon, old movies, and a damsel in distress. If the old world was reborn tomorrow and there were marching bands on Wisconsin Avenue, Howard would still want them to stay inside.

"We're going, Howard. Read me the list."

"Snowshoes, flasks, thermals, pocket heaters, glowsticks, red-tinted ski goggles, a pulk, red boots for Glory."

"What's a pulk?"

"A kind of sled. We can do without it, our board's fine. They probably don't have a pulk anyway. That's specialist."

"Leon didn't recommend one?"

"No."

"You should've paid him more."

Howard smiled his bent smile. "It's pretty mild right now. If we go soon, we might be able to get most of the way there before the weather changes."

"I'll be ready in an hour, Howard."

His face fell, but he didn't argue. In the end, it was closer to two hours when Gloria and Howard walked down the steps from Dorothy's main hatch. They were dressed the same as yesterday but with more equipment and army surplus backpacks. They both had hand crossbows now, in hip holsters. Gloria wasn't very good with it, but it was a sensible precaution against the unknown. As they made their way around the buildings and out of the car park, part of Gloria wondered if she was making a mistake. It was going to be a long hard slog to H Street, then an even harder one back. What choice did she have? Life had to be more than movie nights with Howard and the occasional trip to Safeway.

It would have been great to bring Dorothy, but that was a non-starter. She was an amazing machine, but she was noisy, her 700-horsepower engine could be heard a mile away with nothing else on the road. Sound attracted those things. It was the only point every show agreed on before TV went off the air and the radio died. It was their Golden Rule: No Loud Noises. The infected were probably all dead now, starved or frozen, but they didn't know for sure. Gloria had never seen them in real life, and she didn't want to. Not ever. Better to go on foot than take the risk.

They set off at a steady pace and made good time but it didn't take long for the weather to worsen. As the wind picked up and the snow was churned up into the air, Howard had to navigate with the digital compass. When there was a break in the weather, they found themselves on M Street. Gloria couldn't believe it. It was a ruin. Virtually nothing was left of the places she had loved all her life. Banana Republic looked like it had been blown up and buried. Flo's sidewalk café was unrecognizable. She stopped outside Club Monaco, trying to reconcile her memories with the wreckage. Everything that was beautiful was gone. A hand was sticking up out of the snow and Gloria moved back from it, trying not to think about what else might be under her feet.

"Glory!"

Howard had stopped by a police car, a painted badge on the door with a picture of the Capitol. There was a body in the front seat.

"It's cold, Howard."

"Help me with the door."

"What for?"

"I want to look inside."

Gloria grumbled and pulled from the side while Howard grabbed the top. She leaned away to avoid the broken glass and the dead man's face. Howard took a crowbar from his pack. Once the door was open wide enough, he started pulling at the body. There was no way she was touching it.

"Let's just go, Howard."

He said nothing, breathing hard into his respirator. When he had wrestled the corpse out of the car he leaned in. Gloria looked at the hunched-over body on the snow. It looked small somehow. There was something shameful about what they were doing and she took a step back. Howard straightened, holding up his prize.

"It's a gun," said Gloria.

"A 9mm. There's a shotgun too, but no shells."

"You don't know how to fire a gun."

"You get more with a kind word and a gun than you do with just a kind word."

"What do you want a gun for? Everyone's dead."

"Just in case."

"I'm cold, Howard. Put it away and let's go."

He held it out. "It's for you."

"Me? I don't want it."

"It's easy, like the crossbow. Point it like your finger."

"My finger doesn't kill people."

"His holster won't come off. Put it in your pocket."

"No. It'll go off."

"It only fires if you pull the trigger. There's a little bar."

"I hate guns."

Gloria took the unfamiliar weapon. Though she had always been against guns, there was something about holding it. An excitement. She shook her head.

"You take it, Howard."

She held it out, but he wouldn't take it.

"I'm freezing, Howard. Take it, you can use it to protect me. Be my guardian angel."

That got him and Gloria saw his sideways smile. Tucking the weapon into one of his pockets, they set off again, down what used to be M Street, toward the center of what used to be Washington.

Chapter 5

"What do you mean dead?"

Erlich leaned out of the passenger door. She was a hard-faced woman who didn't smile much. Lang kept it simple. The best lies were always simple.

"We were attacked. Hundreds of infected are coming. We need to go!"

Lang tried to sound breathless, which was easier to fake than fear. The soldier touched her headset.

"Headhunter 1, Headhunter 1, this is Headhunter 3. Over."

Erlich waited then repeated the hail. With no reply, she cursed and started searching through the equipment on the seat beside her.

"We need to go!" shouted Lang.

Erlich tried comms again. "Headhunter 1, Headhunter 1, this is Headhunter 3."

Nothing. Grabbing her submachine gun and helmet, she jumped down to the snow.

"Are you listening to me?" said Lang. "The infected are coming!"

Erlich strapped on her helmet and slammed the door. She didn't bother with the face covering and goggles.

"Tell me what happened," said the soldier, "from the start, don't leave anything out."

"We don't have time!"

Erlich grabbed her by the collar. "Tell me. Now."

Lang thought fast. "There were infected in the building. They surprised us, there were too many. They killed everyone."

"Except you. Where's Copeland and Mapuya?"

"They're dead."

"I said where."

"Microbiology and Immunology."

"Show me."

"I'm not going back there."

The soldier jabbed her weapon into Lang's belly. "Look, lady, I don't trust you one tiny dick's worth. Show me or I shoot you and go anyway."

There was no way Lang could go back. She took a deep breath.

"You can't. The mission, we need to complete the mission." That wasn't going to cut it. She needed more. "I found a cure."

It was a stupid thing to say, you couldn't cure White's Disease. But Erlich didn't know that. The woman glared at her. She kept the weapon against Lang's stomach, then lowered it. Without a word, she pushed past and headed toward the steps. Lang sagged with relief, but it was short-lived. She needed Erlich to drive the M-ATV. If the woman found the others, Lang would face a firing squad. If they even bothered to bring her back. Fuck. Erlich was climbing the steps.

"Wait!" shouted the scientist. "You can't leave me!"

The woman ignored her and kept going. She was almost to the top. Lang had no choice. Unscrewing the suppressor from her pistol, she aimed into the air. The gunshot was incredibly loud, echoing off nearby buildings. Erlich spun around and Lang fired twice more. She kept on shooting until the slide locked back. Not remembering how to reload, she threw the handgun into the snow. Erlich started down again, making her way back. If the soldier didn't kill her, there was a chance Lang might live through this. Movement at the top of the steps caught her eye. Infected, lots of them. One fell, then another, tumbling to the bottom.

Erlich kicked out at the nearest, knocking it over, then blew the head off another. She fired a burst at a third as it reared up. More fell to the bottom of the steps and pushed themselves to their feet. The soldier ran, or as close to running as you could get in the snow, attackers howling in pursuit. Lang had no weapon and couldn't help, so she turned back to the M-ATV. Dozens of infected were charging down Reservoir Road toward her. Shit. Rushing to the passenger door, she missed the handle the first time, then yanked the door open. Lang hauled herself in and pulled it closed. But it didn't close. A hand gripped the edge of the door.

Lang was a biologist and a medical doctor, she knew the heart didn't just stop beating. But right then, it felt like it did. Frantically, she stamped on the hand and pulled the door as hard as she could. More fingers appeared and the gap started to widen. Her boots came down hard, tearing off discolored skin, but she couldn't pry them loose. The door inched open. A face appeared at the window, empty-eyed, skin hanging off. Lang started screaming and kicking with both feet. She was going to die, she knew she was going to die. There was a sharp crack from outside and blood splashed through the opening. The hands disappeared and the door clicked shut.

Lang was trying to breathe as she saw Erlich run around the front of the M-ATV. She climbed into the driver's side.

"Stupid bitch."

Erlich slammed the door and pulled off her helmet.

"We're not leaving. We're going to lose these fuckers, then we're coming back."

She dropped her helmet into the footwell and stabbed the ignition button. They lurched forward, hitting infected and crunching them into the snow. Lang put on her seat belt as she saw more pouring into the road ahead. Where were they coming from? The M-ATV had no trouble smashing through, its huge wheels pulping bodies, but the infected kept on coming. One made it onto the hood, a spindly thing in a torn dress, beating at the windshield. Lang pressed back in her seat as the infected bared its broken teeth and beat at the glass. They bounced over another body and the creature fell off.

Erlich gave the wheel a savage twist, swinging them into an empty side street. They accelerated, making the vehicle shudder over the uneven ground. Once they were free of pursuit, they could slow down again. The engine labored, the electric hum high-pitched and insistent. Lang clung to a metal handle in the roof as the M-ATV shot out of the end of the street and veered right. Erlich stamped on the brakes, snapping Lang's head forward, the seatbelt biting into her shoulder. The soldier's hands tightened on the steering wheel as she stared straight ahead.

A sea of infected filled the roadway. They were everywhere, thousands of them, seething up the sides of the buildings, climbing over each other like ants. More poured from doors and windows to swell the tide that surged toward the M-ATV. How could there be so many? Drones scoured the city for weeks and never found more than a few dozen. All reports said hunger and extreme cold had killed the bulk of the infected population and only a tiny percentage remained. The reports were wrong. Lang was looking at an army of them.

"Drive!" shouted Lang.

"Fuck off."

"If you don't get us out of here, we're dead."

"We're dead anyway. You fucking killed us."

Lang looked at the advancing mass. They must have lain dormant until a new food source presented itself.

"Drive through them."

"There's too many, they'd jam up the wheels."

Lang looked at the rear video feed. "Then go back, there aren't as many at the back."

"We're dead."

Lang grabbed Erlich's arm. "You have to fucking try!"

The soldier shook her off. Lang thought she was going to get a punch in the mouth but instead, Erlich hit the dashboard, over and over again. Her fury faded as she stared through the windshield at infected as far as the eye could see. Erlich grabbed the steering wheel.

"Fuck it."

She put the M-ATV into reverse, slamming into bodies as they backed up. Erlich heaved on the wheel, swinging into a skidding two-point turn. They headed the other way, running over everything in their path. Erlich zigzagged through the thinnest parts of the growing crowd, following the path of least resistance, mashing bodies into the snow. Blood sprayed across the hood and spattered the windshield. A head hit the glass. They were making progress but waves of infected were coming from all directions. The M-ATV began to slow against the press of bodies and there was banging against the armor. The rear feed showed a multitude to their rear. Erlich reached out to a panel on the dashboard with rubberized controls and a screen.

It blinked on. *Common Remotely Operated Weapon Station* flashed up. CROWS. Lang had forgotten the turret. Erlich tapped a few keys. *Automated Mode* appeared, then a screed of technical information; *Target Identified – Target Acquired – Engaging.* Muffled thumps came from the gun on the roof as it started firing, the noise reduced inside by layers of soundproofing. The effect was immediate. High-caliber rounds began tearing bloody chunks from the crowd ahead, ripping them apart. Lang let out a whoop.

"Noise brings more," said Erlich.

"Just shoot them."

"Not enough ammo. All I can do is thin the herd and try to get the fuck out."

The gun changed position and fired. Four-inch brass casings fell like rain past the windows with every burst. It switched to fire in a different direction. Erlich put her foot down and they were moving again.

"Can't let the cocksuckers get too close," said Erlich. "Gun can't hit anything within six feet."

The muted booms stopped, then the big gun started firing again, this time to the rear. On the video feed, she saw infected getting carved into bloody gobbets, body parts disintegrating with every impact. Erlich accelerated, shaking Lang like a rag doll. The windows were covered in gore now. The soldier switched on the wipers and the goo smeared to a rosy tint. They slowed to a crawl and the gun swiveled to fire to the front. Fists hammered on the sides of the M-ATV.

"That's within six feet," said Lang.

"We can handle a few. Too many, we won't be able to move."

"Can we radio for help?"

"QRF's a Super Huey, lady. Sounds like a freight train. Noise draws them dick smokers like flies to shit."

QRF was the Quick Reaction Force, a unit on standby for emergency extractions.

"Can't land, can't use a winch unless we're outside," Erlich went on. "Unless you want to get out in the middle of these fuckers and wave."

The roof-mounted gun was making a path for them, but the sheer amount of empty shells that poured past the window was incredible. Erlich jerked the wheel to the side and Lang grabbed the handrail. Houses gave way to a snowbound embankment and the M-ATV rolled down the slope. The gun moved and fired on its own accord as the computer identified targets all around them. They spun into an empty road going in the opposite direction.

"Did we get away?" asked Lang.

"For now. Gun's dry."

Speeding up, the vehicle shook violently, making Lang want to vomit. Infected appeared ahead, charging from a row of office buildings. They ran right over them. The way ahead was blocked by a wrecked semi, so they ran off the road and plowed through wire fencing and a screen of thickets. They ended up on an access road bordered by trees.

"Dunno where the fuck we are," said Erlich.

Lang didn't see anything she recognized. They rammed a metal gate and approached a wall of green military tents, stretching out in all directions. There were stands for spectators and taller buildings around the perimeter. Erlich edged forward passing a big pavilion. The M-ATV crunched over something hard, then came to a stop.

"Cooper Field," said Lang.

"What?"

"It's a football field for the university. That's student accommodation. This must be a FEMA camp."

"It's an army Field Hospital."

"How do you know?"

"I'm in the army. Have to find a way out."

The terrain was much smoother now and they rolled through little alleys between the tents at a slow walk. After a few minutes, Erlich hit the brakes and opened her door letting in freezing air.

"What are you doing?" asked Lang.

"Looking for a break in the fence line."

Erlich grabbed her weapon and jumped down to the snow. Lang was in no mood to wander around an abandoned army post in these temperatures, so she sat where she was. Erlich didn't close the door, so Lang was left feeling cold anyway. She wished there was a way to ramp up the heating in her camouflage gear. Erlich climbed back in.

"I think it's on the other side, but we can't go around. Have to cut through the tents."

"Maybe we stay here."

"I'd love nothing better than to sit here and play grab-ass with you, lady, but if they find us we've no way out. Got to get to the road."

Erlich edged the M-ATV forward, looking for a way out. They turned left then took another right. The place was a maze.

"Wonder where they went," said Lang.

"Who?"

"The people. "

"Maybe it closed."

"Who closes a hospital in a pandemic?"

"The army."

They paused at a crossroads. There was a big board covered in photos nailed to a post at the junction. A handwritten sign said *Missing*. Even with gaps stripped by the wind, there had to be a thousand pictures up there. Lang looked at the faces. *Have you seen my Danny? Ella Dole – Missing Mom. Don't let my boy be dead*. They drove on. Turning left at the latrines, Erlich jammed on the brakes.

"Fuck."

Infected were pouring between the tents, hundreds of them. The engine whined as Erlich wrenched the wheel right and hit the accelerator through a barracks area. The passage of the M-ATV snapped clotheslines and flattened buckets. Ahead was a larger tent with equipment crates outside. On the video feed, Lang saw a mass of infected behind them. With no way out, Erlich ran straight through the crates and the tent beyond. The collapsed tent blinded them as they barrelled forward. They hit something and the ground fell away.

Lang opened her eyes. The interior of the M-ATV was red with emergency lights. Her shoulder hurt and she struggled to breathe. Blood dripped from her mouth and nose, staining her parka. She tried to move but was still strapped in. Lang hit the release and the seatbelt retracted. Spitting, she used a sleeve to wipe her face. Twisting to check on Erlich, she saw there was little point. The woman lay against the door, head at the wrong angle. Her face was a mask of blood, seeping from the broken parts of her skull. There was a dull thud from the back of the M-ATV. It came again, then there was scraping. Banging followed, spreading out on all sides. The impacts were muted inside the vehicle, like distant drums.

So this was it. Lang didn't think she would die like this, but she hadn't given it a lot of thought. Death was always something that happened to other people. The power was off and so was the heat. Her suit would keep her warm for a few hours, then she would start to freeze. Erlich's gun was there, Lang could make it quick. Or just open the door. Her head hurt and she fished inside the first aid pouch for painkillers. She noticed the edges of the plastic strip were rounded, to stop someone from cutting their thumb. At least she wouldn't bleed to death. Taking out four pills, she swallowed them with water from her canteen.

"What the hell."

She took four more. Lang listened to the pounding on the outside of the M-ATV and wondered how long it would take her to die.

Chapter 6

What remained of 1ˢᵗ Street was broken and burned. Any dignity left to the old buildings was worn well away by the wind. Three figures moved from the ruins, struggling through the snow in bulky black cloaks. The last of them stopped and looked back from under its hood. The Capitol Building was a half-mile behind, framed against the lead-colored sky. Part of the dome had fallen. The figure turned and followed the others. They passed along an avenue with shattered trees jutting up out of the ice. A huge building lay directly ahead, its archways and columns relics of the industrial age. Washington Union Station had been a major transport and logistics hub, with five million people passing through the doors every year. There was no one now.

Wind whickered through the columns as they walked under a 50-foot arch and approached a line of double doors. Statues of knight sentinels stared down at them over heart-shaped shields. The tallest figure stopped outside the middle doors and tried the handle. Metal clacked against metal. It pulled back its hood.

"Who locks their door at the end of the world?"

David Gath was middle-aged and weary. He drew a pistol with a sound suppressor. There was a sharp crack and the glass spidered. He produced a claw hammer from somewhere inside his cloak and bashed until there was a big enough hole to reach inside. With a click, he pulled the door open. They passed through another set of doors into the Great Hall. It was nothing short of majestic. The vaulted roof was studded with octagonal glass and gold, stretching up and out over an expanse of white tiles, statues, and arched latticework windows.

Gath had been here before, but with no people, it looked like a photo. A colonnade stretched away to the left with stores. Starbucks, Chopt, Shake Shack, and more. To the right was a row of doors beneath an old-fashioned clock. Exits on the far wall led to the train platforms, the subway, and the bus terminal. *Tour Tickets, Old Town Trolley* was written in brass on a nearby booth. Above the information desk, gold lettering announced *News, Information, Tours.* The digital departure board was blank. Nobody needed trains anymore and there was nowhere to go.

"Dump the gear, we'll look around," said Gath.

The other figures removed their hoods. Both were younger women. They pulled off their cloaks. Underneath they wore police windbreakers with pistols on their belts. Bags were strapped around their bodies to distribute weight and keep out the cold.

"What are we looking for?" asked Charlie.

She scratched her head. Her hair had been shaved a few weeks ago but was growing back in brown tufts.

"A security office, somewhere with keys."

"They may not use keys," said Chen.

"They'll have backup keys."

Gath was in a gray hiking jacket with a shoulder holster. He lifted one of his soaking running shoes, wishing he had boots. Shrugging off his backpack, he untied the plastic bags. All had a star-shaped logo with *We The Pizza*. They had spent the night in the pizza place, sheltering while they tended to their friend. Neet had been bitten. She never stood a chance, but they hoped anyway. Charlie ended it when the pain became unbearable. That shot was the saddest sound in the world.

"GRACE, bring up Union Station," said Gath.

He raised his forearm. There was a device wrapped around it. A screen came to life with a colored map of the different floors of the station complex.

"It's bigger than I thought."

"It's warmer in here," said Charlie.

"It was built to last. Ticket desks are through there, in the retail concourse. Security isn't marked on the map, but it'll be near the tickets."

"All I heard was retail concourse."

"Keys first, shopping later."

Gath and Charlie started across the open floor to the far doors. Taking a curved sword from a sports bag, Chen slid it through her belt, before jogging to catch up.

"I hope we find candy," said Charlie.

She smiled but it never touched her eyes. Gath pointed ahead to an Alamo Flags booth.

"Go check the gift stall, but I want my cut."

Charlie ran ahead. The booth was a riot of color, stuffed with psychedelic shirts, caps, toys, and every other kind of souvenir. Most of it said *I Heart DC* or *FBI*, with a few superheroes thrown in for good measure. Charlie let out a yelp as she found a bag of Tootsie Rolls. She returned to the others, chewing mightily, and dumped a handful of candy in Chen's outstretched hands.

"Where's mine?" he asked.

Charlie threw him one and moved to the double doors ahead.

"Just one?"

"You're on a diet."

They looked through the glass. The retail concourse was half in shadow, sunlight filtering in from windows set in the ceiling.

"Three levels, all open plan," said Gath. "Give me more."

Charlie threw him another candy. Gath opened both Tootsie Rolls and stuffed them into his mouth. He pushed the doors open and led them out onto a walkway, stopping in front of a bakery. A chalked sign said *Magnolia - Baked Fresh Daily Since 1996*. The shelves were empty. The Body Shop, Bank of America, Wendy's, Avis, McDonald's; all the big-name stores ran off in every direction. Escalators went down to a shadowed food court. Gath could see a central promenade, café tables, stools, and fast-food concessions. Above was a mezzanine with stairs leading up. If the front of Union Station was a landmark, the back was a mall.

"There," said Charlie.

She was pointing farther along on the main concourse. There was a line of kiosks marked for bus services, trains, taxis, the subway, and hotels, glassed in with slots for money.

"That's it, stay frosty," said Gath.

They passed a circular Amtrak Police help desk and moved into an area with banks of seating beside different sets of double doors leading to the tracks. They ran their lights around the walls and storefronts. All the doors leading to the tracks were heavily chained and padlocked.

"Strange," said Gath.

Charlie stopped. "What's strange?"

"They put all these chains on inside doors, but not on the main entrance."

"When we find the keys we can have a look. Maybe that's where they keep all the candy."

Heading along a row of darkened stores, Gath's tactical light landed on another Starbucks. That was the third. Why would they need three Starbucks? There was a Costa Coffee and a Pret too. There was only so much coffee you could drink. They came to a Hotel Chocolat. Now, this was a store you needed a lot of, no question. He would give his left nut for a Cherry Deluxe. Gath shone his light through the window, but there was only dust on the shelves.

"Fuck."

"You're too fat anyway," said Charlie.

They walked on, Chen running a finger across the window of a 7-Eleven. It had been ransacked, with empty boxes and opened cans littering the floor. All that was left were condoms. The Bethesda Travel Center next door had a promotion. A bucket list trip to Jamaica. *Heaven for $999* it said. It sounded nice until he realized Jamaica wasn't a thing anymore. Neither was money. Or heaven.

"*THIS IS THE POLICE.*"

Gath froze. Flashlights snapped on, blinding him. It wasn't the police. The police weren't a thing anymore either. The loudhailer came again.

"*DROP YOUR WEAPONS.*"

He could hear a dog growling.

"*DROP YOUR WEAPONS OR WE FIRE.*"

Gath didn't know what to do, but he didn't have much choice. He threw his pistol off to the side and the others did the same. Chen's sword followed a moment later, clattering across the tiles. He tried to shield his eyes against the light.

"*ON YOUR KNEES, LACE YOUR FINGERS BEHIND YOUR HEAD.*"

It sounded like the police, but it couldn't be.

"*DO IT NOW.*"

They knelt and did as instructed. Two men moved forward holding flashlights. They were hard to see in the glare but seemed to be wearing armor. Claws scrabbled on the floor. The light moved from Gath's face and he started to get his vision back. He saw the dog first, a German Shepherd in a harness, straining at the leash. Its handler wore a black helmet, gas mask, and hard-shell riot gear. *Police* was stamped in white on his chest plate. The man hefted his weapon, a bulky carbine with a thick rotating magazine. He had a loudhailer dangling from his belt. The second man in the same armor patted Gath down. He didn't do a very good job.

A banging came from one of the sets of doors leading to the tracks. The man searching him stopped and aimed his flashlight at the chains sealing the entrance to Track 4. They rattled but held firm. Something was out there and it didn't take much imagination to guess what. Banging started at the doors to Track 5. The man moved away a few steps, yanked off his helmet and gas mask, and vomited. He was shockingly young, like a high school kid. The man with the dog let go of the leash, zip-tying Gath's hands. The German Shepherd trotted over to the pile of sick, sniffed, then started to lick it. The harness said *Amtrak Police, Do Not Pet.*

"Ozzy!" called the dog handler. "Get away!"

The young man wiped his face. "They heard us."

"Don't matter. Pick up your helmet and see to the women."

Gath watched the dog. It didn't look very fierce. It tilted its head and stared at him with big brown eyes. Chen and Charlie knelt beside Gath. The man with the dog walked out to stand in front of his prisoners, the flashlight moving slowly from one to the other.

"You broke my door."

No one said anything.

"Don't take kindly to looters."

"We're not looters," said Charlie.

The light snapped to her and the man came closer, running the beam up and down her police windbreaker.

"You sure as heck ain't cops, missy. District of Columbia Code, article 22-1406, Impersonation of a Police Officer, punishable by imprisonment in the District Jail or penitentiary not exceedin' 180 days. Looters and lawbreakers, any way you slice it."

"The uniforms aren't stolen, officer."

"I know looters when I see looters."

"I was working with the Beaumont Police Department."

"Never heard of it."

"It's in Texas."

"Figures. Don't talk like you're from Texas."

"If you give me time, I can explain."

"Lies take time, missy. Truth's quick."

"I'm a federal agent."

The man hesitated.

"Homeland Security," Charlie went on. "I worked out of the Austin Field Office on assignment with Beaumont PD."

"Don't look like a Fed to me. Just a girl in someone else's coat."

"There's a badge in my pocket. If you free my hands, I'll show you."

"Ain't gonna be any hands gettin' freed."

He walked away and spoke quietly to the younger policeman who approached Charlie. He seemed reluctant.

"Which side is your badge?" he asked.

"Inside right pocket."

Fresh banging started at the track doors, and they all turned to look.

"Get on with it," said the one in charge.

The young man set down his headgear and held up the flashlight. He had one hand free for the search and he used it to pull down the zipper on Charlie's windbreaker.

"Sorry," he said.

He opened the inner pocket, going to great effort not to brush against Charlie's breast. He took out a black leather wallet and opened it. There was a gold and blue shield with an eagle crest on it. Opposite the badge was an ID card.

"Department of Homeland Security." The young man read. "Special Agent Carlotta M. Giordano, Office of Intelligence and Analysis."

He aimed the flashlight at her face and then down at the ID.

"It's her."

Gath watched the dog's breath misting in the air as they waited for the reaction. He had the awful feeling that revealing Charlie's identity was a mistake. The policeman tugged the dog's leash and slung his weapon. Reaching up, he pulled off his helmet and gas mask. He was old and bald, his head shining with sweat. His expression was grim, like a judge passing a death sentence. Then he gave a wide, gap-toothed grin.

"Thank God!"

Chapter 7

It was pitch black when Prashad opened her eyes. She had fallen asleep. Terror couldn't last forever. Eventually, the body shut down, even if the reason for fear remained. She checked her watch. It would be getting dark outside. Her shoulders ached and the box she sat on smelled like a dog. Being afraid for her life was a new sensation. There had been another feeling too. Excitement. That was the biology of fear. The amygdala alerted the nervous system, releasing cortisol and adrenaline. She felt more alive in that run from the infected than at any other time in her life. A marine she was dating told her the biggest rush in the world was to be shot at and survive. He was right.

Operation Headhunter was dead. Lang killed it when she shot Dubchek. Though the woman didn't know it, she had also killed Prashad's prospects of promotion. Her superiors would not be happy that Lang had escaped. Oh well, at least she was alive. That ought to count for something. When the stakes were life and death, success was an easy thing to measure. Prashad had been on leave at her home in Brentwood when the outbreak had begun. Her parents told her not to return to Aegis, it was too dangerous. They were always criticizing and she was sick of it. She caught the first transport back to DC. Prashad's parents never criticized her again. Brentwood had been firebombed with the rest of LA.

Copeland was furious when Lang disappeared, but it was no surprise to Prashad. She had been warned that Lang was looking for something. What it was, her superiors didn't know, but it was important and they wanted it. Human Research and Engineering was always playing second fiddle to Weapons and Materials Research. Not anymore. Prashad's orders were to get whatever Lang was after, by any means necessary. Team expendable. Dubchek was her Head of Section, but he was weak. If Prashad brought back the prize, she would take his place. If Lang didn't come back, she wouldn't be missed. Neither would Dubchek.

They searched Microbiology and Immunology with no results, then headed to Biochemistry, Lang's old department. Getting turned around in the warren of corridors and hundreds of rooms, they had difficulty covering enough ground. Copeland told them to split up and assigned areas for each to search, but Prashad ignored him and struck out on her own. She found a sign saying *Research Wing*. That's where the woman would be. Though Prashad didn't know Lang, she knew she was a parasite, building her reputation on the backs of others. Whatever she was looking for wasn't her own work, or she would have copies of it. Lang was here to steal someone else's.

She heard a distant banging. Moving toward the sound, she headed down a hallway and then moved through an open-plan reading area. Someone was up ahead, in one of the branching corridors. A light bounced about as a man kicked a door. Copeland, it had to be. Dubchek was too fat to kick anything. Prashad moved closer hugging the wall, not wanting to be seen. Copeland booted the damaged door off its hinges and pushed inside. She ran forward and peered through the doorway. It was a lounge of some kind, with tables, chairs, and lockers.

The Sergeant stood on the far side, pointing his submachine gun through a smashed window. She saw Dubchek on the floor, blood staining the front of his parka. Copeland shouted Lang's name.

"What happened?" asked Prashad, moving into the room.

Copeland didn't turn. "Bitch shot him."

If Lang was going around shooting people, she must be after something really big.

"Can't see her on the Merson," he went on. "She's either out of range or this thing's shit."

"They said it doesn't work very well inside."

"I'll have to climb out and look. Or you could do it, you'd fit through the hole."

"Not my job, Sergeant."

Copeland turned to look at Prashad for the first time, anger getting the better of him.

"Someone's dead, that means I'm in charge. If I need you to go look, you'll go fucking look."

He turned back and yelled Lang's name. It was a waste of time. She was hardly going to come back. A figure appeared at the window, but it wasn't Lang. It reached through, skinless fingers latching onto the Sergeant's shoulder. More figures appeared, dragging him out through the window. Copeland fired a few shots but teeth bit into him, blood spurting over his parka. Shards of glass sliced his back and fingernails raked his face. He screamed.

Prashad raised her pistol, then lowered it. If she started shooting, they might notice her. One of the attackers fell into the room, writhing on the carpet, trying to stand. Despite herself, Prashad was fascinated. The man was obscene, skin rotting, a missing eye giving him a permanent leer. She could smell him from across the room. Fetid, fecal, it made her skin crawl. Prashad reconsidered using her weapon, but another fell in and the first got to its feet, hissing. She backed away, slowly reversing through the door. The lock was smashed, and it couldn't be closed. The infected charged and she sprinted off down the hallway.

Prashad's flashlight was useless when she ran, flickering against the walls and floor as she pumped her arms. Running blind was almost as terrifying as the snarls of the infected chasing her. A practical child, she was never a believer in monsters. There was no evidence. Now, with the evidence a few yards behind her, she was a believer. Prashad was fit but she couldn't run flat out forever. She needed to hide. Hurtling through a small reading area, she pulled a bookshelf down as she went. The crash was followed by a series of bone-jarring thuds. She toppled a display cabinet in the next hallway, then ran on. Prashad was sure she was close to the laboratories.

Speeding up, she saw the single green light of the lab door Lang had unlocked. It slid back and she stepped inside, pressing the panel to lock it. But it didn't lock. Fuck. She panned her light over the stools, benches, and shelves. At the back, there were fume hoods, cabinets, and a safety shower with no curtain. Prashad ran to the back, wrenched open a cabinet, and pulled out stacks of plastic trays. Squeezing inside to sit on a cardboard box, she turned off her flashlight and held the door closed. Running feet and muffled grunts came from the corridor. The door slid open. Footsteps came close, something kicked the trays. Prashad's grip on the door tightened. Time stood still until the door swished open again, then closed.

That was hours ago. It was amazing what you could get used to when you had no choice. Prashad put her ear to the door of the cabinet but heard nothing. Her legs were cramping, and her left foot had fallen asleep. More importantly, she needed to pee. She pushed the door open an inch. There was nothing to see in the unlit lab and no reek of unwashed bodies, only dust and the astringent smell of all laboratories. Prashad had grown up with it. From the Grade 4 science fair to the Lederberg Award at Stanford, it meant an orderly existence, logical and precise, the way everything should be. That is what her life had been until two months ago. Right then she wanted nothing more than to be back in the lab at Aegis, surrounded by the work she loved.

Prashad got out of the cabinet and stretched. It was hard to see but she didn't want to use the flashlight. Half the wall was glass and anything could be out there. She stood, letting the minutes tick by. There was a blob of black on the floor by a bench. Prashad reached out and gave it a quick kick. A stool. She really needed to pee. Unclipping her belt, she pulled down the camouflage pants and squatted. Gooseflesh pricked in the cold air but she didn't care. The relief of emptying her bladder was bliss. She found a tissue, dried off, and pulled up her pants. Seeing nothing through the glass, she pressed the panel and the door slid open.

Prashad had to get out of this place and back to the M-ATV. If it was still there. The driver was supposed to wait, but not this long. If it had left, she was screwed. Prashad took a sip of water from her canteen and then headed left, back the way she had come. No point going the same way as the infected. The soldier at the front door was either gone or dead by now. Her best bet was going out the Faculty Office window and walking around to the front. As exciting as running from the infected was, it only made you feel alive if you got away.

The halls were dark but she didn't want to risk a light. She felt her way along the wall, pistol aimed at nothing. Careful but incredibly slow. Prashad had to avoid plant pots and displays as she went. After ten minutes of this, she decided to risk a light. At first, she kept it aimed at the floor, so she could see where she was putting her feet and there was less chance of it being seen. Then she started shining it ahead. After all, if there was anything nasty, she wanted to see it before she walked into it. Prashad picked up the pace.

The next hallway had smears along the wall, and she was glad she didn't have to touch it. She moved around an up-ended table and stepped over soil and dried leaves from a broken pot. She came to a waiting area she didn't recognize and found corpses. Three lay on the floor, one was propped up against an armchair. The faces were misshapen, the flesh discolored. Infected, shot hours ago. The soldier lived long enough to kill a few, or maybe the driver came looking. Either way, they weren't here now.

Giving the bodies a wide berth, she continued. It had taken her 30 minutes already, so she decided to move faster. Jogging to the next turning, she slowed to peek around with her light. Nothing. She ran to the next corner and did the same. Before long she was back in Microbiology. Prashad leaped over a fallen lamp. She was getting cocky but she still stopped to look around the next corner. Her light fell on two men, standing beside a half-empty water cooler, facing away. One wore a uniform, the other a coat, his fat frame making it bulge. She pulled back. They must have seen the light. Prashad pointed her weapon at the corner and waited.

When nothing happened, she moved to the far wall and sidestepped until she could see the men again. They didn't move, just looked toward another hallway. Prashad could smell them now. The sewerage and dead thing stink she had smelled before. She was really glad she hadn't run right into them. The one in a uniform spasmed and turned around. He was a cop, moving slowly like he had forgotten how. His shirt was clean with an unblemished tie. Just another day on patrol, dear. The face, on the other hand, was something else.

The man's skin was dry and cracked like old paper, the lips had been gnawed away. Then there were the eyes. Prashad tried not to be afraid. The watery white eyes looked like poached eggs. She knew it was Final Stage Eye Decomposition, the white irises caused by a lack of oxygen to the lens, cornea, and aqueous humor. Knowing was one thing, but seeing it this close was another. The policeman made a choking noise, like a broken pipe. This caught the attention of the fat man, who also turned. He was spattered with gore, most of his face had been ripped away.

They charged. Prashad jerked the trigger, missing them both. She fired again, hitting the policeman in the shoulder, spinning him into a coffee table. The fat man was close now and she shot him in the chest. He rocked back on his heels but kept coming. Prashad fired again and turned his face to hamburger. He hit the floor with a wet sound but the policeman was getting up. These PIKE rounds were supposed to kill these fuckers with one shot. She aimed and hit the cop in the head, shredding his face and spattering the wall with gore.

She was shaking and she sat on the side of a couch. Adrenaline, she knew, but she still had to wait for it to pass. Part of the dead cop's brain hung out of his skull. Normal brain matter was soft like jelly. White's Disease made holes in it and turned the texture to putty. Taking off her goggles, she wiped organic material onto her pants. Prashad bent over the body in case there was anything of use on his belt. Cuffs, pepper spray, but no gun holster. The badge said *Georgetown University Police Department*. Maybe university cops didn't use guns. Maybe he'd be alive if they did. Prashad took out a water bottle, drank, and then poured some over her goggles.

Not far now. Prashad moved with more caution. She kept the flashlight and gun aimed ahead, scanning for movement. Entering a hallway decorated with old trophy cabinets, she approached the reading area that led to the Faculty Office. She stopped in her tracks. A lady's dress shoe was sticking out from the next corner. Prashad moved to the far side of the hallway to keep her distance, seeing more and more of the reading area as she went. Her light ran across at least a dozen bodies. the bodies littered the place. The shoe was on the foot of a dead woman in an evening dress. She was mangled, the tissue blown apart by multiple PIKE rounds. The stink was terrible.

Prashad picked her way through the grisly scene and headed on to the Faculty Office. The doors were open and she shone in her flashlight Dubchek was still on the floor, but there were dead infected too. No sign of Copeland. He wouldn't have been eaten, the infected didn't fully consume a body. No one knew why, but current thinking related it to oxygen levels in the blood. The window in the office had little glass now and snow had blown in, lying in piles on the carpet. Prashad ran her light over the coffee tables, armchairs, couches, and lockers at the back. There was even a breakfast bar.

Still couldn't find Copeland's body. The man couldn't have survived, he had been ripped apart. He had a submachine gun and the Merson. They would significantly improve her chances of survival. A chill touched her and she turned, shining her light around the room. Nothing. Well, nothing apart from the bodies. She moved to Dubchek to take his ammunition, but it was already gone. Prashad shone her light on his fat face. He wouldn't be missed. Walking towards the breakfast bar, she stepped over a naked woman covered in old bites. Her skin was so frostbitten it looked like she had been burnt.

A Bunn Speed Drip Coffee Maker sat on the countertop. On shelves at the back were dishes, glasses, and a kettle. Something moved behind her and she spun, pistol raised. She knocked a cup onto the floor. When it smashed, she fired by reflex. Prashad tried to control her breathing as she searched with her flashlight. A piece of paper had been blown from a table by a gust from the window. She stared down at it on the floor. *WE'RE FUCKED* was scrawled in black Sharpie.

"Get a hold of yourself," she said out loud.

It made her feel better to hear a voice, even if it was her own. Taking a deep breath, she took a sip from her canteen and hooked it back on her belt. She wished it was vodka. There was another sound and she raised her flashlight. A man in a bloody white parka rushed at her. Prashad tried to fire but he grabbed the pistol and twisted it up. Two shots hit the ceiling before the iron grip dragged her close. All Prashad could smell was death and decay. She screamed.

Chapter 8

"Sergeant William McCord, Ma'am, Amtrak Police. Call me Bill."

The young cop cut off her zip-ties, then moved to the others. Charlie stood up, rubbing her wrists.

"I'm Charlie, this is David and Chen."

The old officer waited while the group picked up their weapons. More banging came from the track doors.

"What's out there?" she asked.

"Nothing we need to fuss over," said McCord, then bent to pet the dog. "This here's Ozzy. Say hi Ozzy!"

The German Shepherd growled and McCord stroked its ears.

"Don't worry about old Ozzy, Ma'am, he's all bark and slobbers."

"You guys have someplace we could talk?" asked Gath. "Somewhere quiet?"

McCord winked. "Follow me."

He took them along the retail concourse, passing UNIQLO and a Dunkin Donuts with empty shelves.

Gath drew level with the young officer. "What's your name?"

"Oh, Nix. Sorry."

"Nick?"

"Nix. N, I, X."

They came to a door marked *Operations* beside a map of the station. Ignoring the security panel, McCord jangled a bunch of keys before sliding one into the lock. Inside was a large changing room lined with lockers and bare wooden benches, with more exits leading off. Two small camping lamps meant they didn't need flashlights. Nix closed the door and pressed a stud to lock it. Setting his headgear on a bench, McCord leaned down to unhook Ozzy's leash from its harness. The dog immediately ran to the newcomers to give them a good sniff. Charlie smiled and stroked the dog's neck. Chen kept her distance. Nix unstrapped his riot gear.

"I hate wearing this shit."

"Watch your mouth," said McCord.

Nix didn't reply and continued to pull off the hard-shell armor. He wore a baggy police uniform underneath.

"Those doors won't hold forever," said Gath.

The old cop didn't look at him. "They settle when they ain't riled."

"What if they get in?"

"Doors are steel-framed, half-inch chains. If you ain't a Fed, what are you?"

"Air Force."

"Figures."

McCord didn't take off his armor. He pointed at the nearest door.

"Control Room's in there, rest of Operations is wash facilities, rec room, cafeteria, kitchen, storage, and maintenance. Police Headquarters is on the Mezzanine Level, down here's mostly service staff."

Gath gestured to the rows of lockers. "How many service staff are there?"

"None."

The policeman pushed through the door, holding it open for the others. Gath walked into a small security room dominated by a wide window looking out onto a long row of ticket desks and the retail concourse.

"Home sweet home," said McCord. "One-way armor glass, with a bird's-eye view."

Charlie picked up a crumpled magazine from a low coffee table. It said *Field & Stream*, a picture of a man fishing at sunset on the cover.

"Very cozy."

She put it back down. The place was lit by more portable lamps. Dozens of blank display screens ran in rows on either side of the glass and a control board stretched the length of the room. There were swivel chairs, a coffee table, filing cabinets, a rack of two-way radios, and two other doors. An old CD player sat on one of the chairs, a police jacket over the back. A few used plates and coffee mugs were scattered around.

"It's not much, but it's safe," said McCord. "Even if one of them things got onto the concourse, they're not gettin' in here."

Gath rubbed his chin. "What are the chances of them getting onto the concourse?"

"Zero."

"How many cops do you have?"

"Amtrak's got 452 sworn officers, 212 operating out of Union Station."

"How many are left?"

"One."

"There are two of you."

"Kid ain't police."

Nix gave an uncomfortable smile.

"But I'm still here like I was told," said the old man. "Place is in one piece. More or less."

"How many infected are out there?"

"Too many."

They stood looking at each other, no one really knowing what to say.

"What now?" asked McCord.

Gath smiled. "I guess that's up to you, Sarge."

"I did my duty. What's next?"

Charlie and Gath looked at each other.

"We don't know what you mean," said Charlie.

"I was ordered to hold until relieved. Now you're here. So, what's next?"

"I'm sorry, Bill. We're not your relief."

McCord frowned. "But you're Federal."

"We were just looking for somewhere to hide. We're survivors, like you."

"I'm not a survivor, I'm police. Who sent you?"

"No one sent us," said Gath. "There is no one. It's all gone."

"What about the army?"

"There is no army. No police, no government, no people. We've been on the road for days, only met a couple of survivors. Everyone else was infected or hostile. I'm sorry."

The old man stared at him, uncomprehending, then he sat on a chair. Nix waited by the door, eyes wide. To give himself something to do, he went around the room picking up dirty dishes, then left without a word. McCord reached out to pet the German Shepherd. The dog licked his hand, and he looked up, face ashen.

"You'll be needing beds."

The old cop stood and opened one of the doors. Inside was dark, but there was enough light from the Control Room to see the outline of bunk beds.

"For split shifts. There's a place in maintenance for the women. Nothin' fancy. Toilets and showers are through the locker room. No hot water. There's a bit of dried food but all we can do is boil stuff, it ain't great. Mostly we eat cookies. You got food?"

"Not much."

"Figures."

McCord went to the other door. Opening it with a key, he turned on another camping lamp. The room was small, the walls covered with cages and racks, a couple of crates on the floor. There were tear gas canisters, pepper spray, and two riot helmets. Another of the high-caliber weapons the old man carried hung on a hook.

"Not much left after everyone cleared out. Got a shotgun but no shells. Two nine mils, but no ammo."

Gath lifted the big weapon by its strap. "What's this?"

"A Milkor. Riot gun, non-lethal, fires baton rounds."

"Any use against the infected?"

"What do you think?"

"I think you're lucky we came quietly. What's in the crates?"

"Tasers and flares. More baton rounds."

The policeman turned off the lamp and closed the door. Nix was sitting in a swivel chair wearing the police windbreaker that had been hanging on the back. He was even less like a cop now, painfully thin in the too-big jacket, arms wrapped around himself for warmth. While it wasn't freezing in the Control Room, it certainly wasn't warm. The dog was lying beside him, watching events with mild curiosity. McCord bent and scratched its ears.

"Ozzy ain't a sworn peace officer neither, are you Oz? He's mine, got special permission to bring him in. Couldn't leave him." He straightened. "If you're feelin' the chill, we can use the heater. Only one bottle of propane left, though."

"How do you charge the lamps?"

"Batteries. Got a load from a Family Dollar on the promenade."

Gath walked to the blank display screens. "The station must have a generator."

"We got three, but they don't work."

"Maybe I could take a look for you?"

"They're out on the tracks."

Where all the infected were. Gath sighed. When Nix came back, McCord gestured for his visitors to take the available seats. The young man sat on the floor beside the dog.

"So, you're Air Force," said McCord.

"Me and Captain Chen are pilots."

"If she's a Captain, what are you?"

"A colonel."

"Figures. We're a bit short of planes, Colonel. Where's your uniform?"

"Underneath."

"You're wearin' tennis shoes."

"We're part of the space program, soft shoes are more practical."

The policeman's eyes narrowed. "Space?"

"We're Air Force officers attached to NASA."

"You're astronauts?" asked Nix.

"Yes."

"Easy to say," said McCord.

Gath stood up, unclipped GRACE from his arm then set it on the chair. He shrugged off his shoulder holster and unfastened his belt before unzipping his hiking jacket. It was uncomfortably cold. He was left standing in his blue flight suit, complete with the US flag, NASA logo, and his Expedition 70 patch. *Gath* was written on the left breast below spreading wings.

Nix broke into a smile, but McCord scowled.

"Gath's where the Philistines came from."

Nix pointed to the computer.

"What's that?"

"GRACE, say hello."

"*Hello, Sergeant McCord and Mr. Nix. I am NASA's Global Recognition and Communications Environment. Please call me GRACE. Nice to meet you.*"

The computer spoke with a soft, female voice.

McCord was unhappy. "How come it knows who we are?"

"GRACE can hear and see better than we can," said Gath.

"Can I touch it?" asked Nix.

Gath smiled and the young man moved to the device, running a finger tentatively over the screen.

"But there's no network anymore."

"We have our own. It's not connected to the web but the database is pretty good. Try it."

"How?"

"Ask her a question."

Nix thought about it. "Where are we?"

"*We are in Washington Union Station, Massachusetts Ave NE, Washington, DC.*"

McCord shook his head. "Even an idiot would know that. Ask it who's the Chief of the APD."

"*Doyle Samuel Dotson III is Chief of the Amtrak Police Department.*"

The old cop didn't say anything, but the expression on his face said GRACE was correct. Gath put his hiking jacket back on and clipped GRACE onto his arm.

"Why are you in DC? How did you get here?" asked Nix.

"That's a long story. We were on the International Space Station when the outbreak started."

"You were up there? When?"

"Until two days ago. We lost communications, we didn't know what was going on."

McCord stared at Chen. "You too?"

She stood up and took off her jacket and the police sweatshirt. The clothes had been Neet's but Charlie had insisted Chen take them to keep her warm. Underneath was the top half of a flight suit like Gath's. *Chen* was on the name tape and instead of a US flag, there was a red one with gold stars.

"Wait a minute," said McCord. "That ain't our flag."

Gath had been waiting for this. "Captain Chen is in the Chinese Air Force."

"Chinese? Why's there Chinamen on our space station?"

"It's an international space station. We had crew members from Europe, Russia, and Japan too. The Chinese have their own space station, but we invited Captain Chen to join our crew as an observer."

Nix stood up and held his hand out. "Nice to meet you, Captain Chen."

"Nice to meet you too, Nix," said Chen, shaking hands.

McCord was glaring at Gath. "Russians?"

"It was an international crew."

"After what they did?"

"My crew wasn't involved."

"They're murderers, that's what they are. I hope all them godless Commies are left to rot in the same hole."

No one mentioned the Russian government hadn't been Communist for over 30 years. The Chinese were still Communists, but Chen didn't seem to take offense.

Nix changed the subject. "Why did you come back? You were safe up there."

"Being safe wasn't enough. We didn't want our scientists up there running experiments when they could be down here saving lives."

"You a scientist?" asked McCord.

"No."

He pointed at Chen. "What about you?"

She shook her head.

"Then where are all these scientists?"

"They didn't make it," said Gath.

"Figures."

Gath was getting fed up with the old man.

"Why's she here?" said McCord, pointing a thumb at Chen. "I've nothin' against Chinamen, but this ain't her country."

"She's a friend, Bill," said Charlie.

McCord nodded and gave a gappy smile. "Well, even if she ain't a scientist, it's mighty Christian of her to help." He turned to Chen. "Do they have Christians in your neck of the woods, Miss?"

"We have all religions in China," said Chen, "but not the government. Our government has no religion."

"Just like here. They only worship money. Plague did one good thing. No more politicians. You want coffee? We have a kettle, runs on batteries."

Charlie whistled. "Coffee would be great."

Nix got the message and left to make the drinks. Charlie asked where the toilet was and followed Nix out. They sat there in silence.

"Tell me about these hostiles," McCord said to Gath.

"Why do you want to know?"

"Are they still after you?"

"What do you mean?"

"C'mon Colonel. I'm old, not dead. You were on the road for days, your scientists were killed, and you were lookin' for somewhere to hide."

Gath rubbed his chin. "They're still after us."

"Who?"

"Private military contractors."

"Mercenaries. Scum."

"They're called Lexington, well-trained and well-equipped. We had a job to do and they didn't want us to do it."

"They know you're here?"

"I don't think so."

McCord considered what he had heard. "What job?"

"Find a scientist, give her something."

"More scientists. Did you find her?"

"No."

The old cop scratched his ear. "You think they'll come lookin' for you?"

"Eventually."

"Then I figure we better be ready."

Gath's opinion of McCord went up a few notches.

"Can you tell us what actually happened?" asked Gath. "We were out of contact and don't know how it all fell apart. We know there was a bomb and the outbreak, but no details."

"Not much else to know. There was a quarantine."

"In DC?"

"Everywhere. Soldiers all over the place, but guns don't stop plague."

McCord shifted in his chair.

"I've been around, Colonel. Never seen the like. Them streets were demented. A demon got into those people, lootin' and burnin' and killin'. That was before the infected. City went straight to perdition. I worked seven-day weeks, better than bein' at home. Got picked up and taken home in a SWAT truck. Had three locks on my door, kept the drapes closed. Me and Ozzy watched TV, with the sound up so we couldn't hear the screams. Westerns, mostly. We love Westerns, don't we boy?"

Ozzy's tail started wagging, but he stayed curled on the floor. Nix and Charlie returned carrying mugs and passed them out. Sitting back down on the floor with some water, Nix petted the dog and Charlie picked up an old CD case.

"Willie Nelson?"

"Musical genius," said McCord. "Don't break it."

Charlie set it down. The coffee was only instant, but the smell made Gath's mouth water. It was in an Amtrak Police mug, an eagle on one side. The other had *I'm Off Duty, Save Yourself.*

"Where was FEMA?" Gath asked McCord.

"Them boys couldn't dig half a hole. Saw one FEMA truck the whole time and it had no wheels."

"I saw FEMA," said Nix.

Everyone looked at him and he turned red.

"What are we talking about?" asked Charlie.

Gath sipped his coffee. "The Sergeant was just telling us what happened during the outbreak."

"'I saw another sign in heaven,'" quoted McCord, "seven angels with seven plagues, which are the last, for with them the wrath of God is finished.'"

They digested this as they drank their coffee. The dog whined and the young man petted him.

"When did you see FEMA?" Gath asked Nix.

"At the end."

"Can you tell it from the start?"

Nix swallowed. "I can try."

It took a while for the young man to gather himself, then he began.

"It was December 10th, we had an exhibition. I'm an artist."

McCord snorted.

"Go on," said Gath.

"We had a showing in Dupont Underground, part of the old streetcar system turned into an exhibition center. The piece was different live news shows projected onto the walls. Then it changed, all the networks reporting the same thing. Bomb at Fort Detrick. There was smoke and people were shouting. The feed was so raw they didn't have time to cut the swearing. Burned corpses on the ground, bits of bodies. We thought it was terrorists until they kicked out the Russian Ambassador. No one said why."

"Because they did it, Godless heathens," said McCord.

"A lot of people said it was the Russians but the government didn't. The President wouldn't answer the question, he just called for calm."

"Democrats is worse than Commies," said the old cop.

"War was all people could think about," Nix went on. "Russia, North Korea, Iran, China," he smiled an apology to Chen. "Then came the disease. That was different. It didn't hit the news all at once, it was slow. It started on social media with a few weird reports, people saying it was a disease from immigrants or chemicals in the water or ebola."

"Or both," said McCord. "Commies are up to all sorts. Shoulda nuked them when Reagan was in office."

"Then it hit prime time," said Nix, "there were pics, videos. People were getting sick and going crazy, attacking each other in the street. Everyone said stuff but no one knew anything, especially the government. It moved too fast. People with lumps on their skin and bite marks were all over Twitter and TikTok. A cop was talking to Morning Joe, his partner was on a stretcher in the background and he bit one of the EMTs. The cop had to shoot him, his own partner, live on air."

Nix was reliving the moment and he had to pause.

"It's OK," said Charlie. "Take your time."

He smiled, then the smile faded. "They brought in quarantine the same day. One minute we were free, the next we weren't. The army was at airports and train stations. Guys in hazmat suits started taking people away."

"What about evacuations?"

"Where you gonna go?" asked McCord. "You can't evacuate big cities. Sure, they cleared out Gainesville and places like that, but they're tiny. DC's three-quarter of a million. No camp big enough for that."

"That's when I saw FEMA," said Nix. "They opened an office at the PNC Bank in Dupont Circle. They were giving out flyers and supplies, trying to calm everyone down. The gallery was closed by then but we got the keys so we could meet. By Christmas, we were living there. Streets weren't safe anymore. Soldiers were shooting looters, cops were gone. Gangs were robbing people and hitting stores. It was cold and getting colder. We had a little generator, enough to keep us alive and run a stove. So we sealed ourselves in. The roof shook when they brought the tanks in. By New Year, the President was down in his bunker. We heard he was dead."

"Not dead," said McCord. "Just a Democrat."

"The TV was emergency broadcasts," said Nix. "The net went down so we used an old FM radio. We ran through the frequencies every night. People asking for help, begging. Once we heard banging on the door, but we didn't open it. We didn't have much. If we let them in, we'd all starve. So, we just sat there and hoped they'd go away. The banging went on for ages, then it stopped. We left them out there. We knew it was hell, but we left them out there anyway."

Chapter 9

Two lanes of cars stretched as far as the eye could see, frozen to the road. Pennsylvania Avenue had been America's Main Street, lined with landmarks, and packed with visitors from across the world. Now it was a cemetery. Sometimes, Gloria wished she hadn't survived, that she had died with everybody else. Her head hurt and she steadied herself on a car door. Something was sticking out of the snow on the hood, something green, the only piece of color for miles around. She reached out and grabbed it, wiping away the frost. *Rolling Rock, Premium Beer, Extra Pale.* There was an inch of liquid frozen at the bottom. Gloria missed beer. She missed everything.

Howard was ahead, struggling against the snow and a freshening wind. He was walking between the rows of stationary traffic where the snow was thinnest. His orange parka made him look like a pumpkin, and she managed a giggle. He turned to see if she was alright and she waved a hand to show she was fine. Gloria set the bottle back; it had made it this far. Good luck little bottle! She started walking again, each step through the drifts making her head pound.

She hoisted the scarf to shield her eyes from the glare. Sun reflected off the neverending white, driving her crazy.

Howard moved on, knowing better than to come back to check on her. Gloria had used some colorful language the last time he asked. She didn't need a man to take care of her and if she did, it wouldn't be Howard. They passed the Ristorante la Perla. She had been a couple of times, but only when a guy was paying. Its brickwork was scorched and pockmarked, the windows shattered. The blue canopy was shredded and hung down like confetti. Her head was getting worse. She would need to find sunglasses somewhere.

It galled her to have to admit weakness to Howard, but a migraine was worse than a blow to her dignity. Sometimes necessity was greater than pride, that's why kneeling was invented. Kneeling sounded like bliss right about then, and Gloria sank into the snow. There was a moment of relief, then the pain returned. Howard grunted back to her and she held up a hand.

"Go away, it's just a headache."

He rooted around in his pouches. "I have ibuprofen."

"I don't need ibuprofen, I need sunglasses."

"I don't have sunglasses. I gave you the respirator, but you didn't like wearing it." He rapped his faceplate. "It's anti-glare."

"Give me the pills and go away."

She took out her water bottle while Howard wrestled with the strip of Motrin. They weren't designed for thick gloves.

"Give them here," said Gloria.

Her tighter gloves defeated the wrapping. One pill fell but she managed to get three others into her mouth. As she swigged her water she began to regret kneeling. Her ski pants were waterproof, but it was still damned cold.

"I don't think there are any sunglass places nearby, Glory. Maybe they have them in 7-Eleven."

"There's a Trader Joe's. It's not far."

"That's my girl."

Gloria wanted to snap at him, but she couldn't talk. Getting to her feet, they continued on. It took another ten minutes before they approached the turn to Trader Joe's. They found a gap where the cars weren't bumper-to-bumper and walked down 25th Street. It was picturesque, fringed with trees and quaint apartment buildings. Trader Joe's wasn't far. The red lettering on the awning was covered in ice, but the store seemed untouched. The automatic doors were closed but the shutters weren't down. Good old Trader Joe. Gloria didn't know if Trader Joe was an actual person but her headache was receding now, so she warmed to him anyway.

She pushed on the glass but the doors wouldn't budge. Gloria gave them a kick and regretted it as the throb returned. Fuck you sideways, Trader Joe. Howard took a few minutes to force the doors apart using a tool from his collection. They jammed after a couple of feet, but that was plenty.

"Haven't been to a Trader Joe's in years," he said. "Just when I thought I was out, they pull me back in."

Gloria fit through the gap with her pack still on. It was warmer inside out of the wind. The place was dim and smelled of neglect. She took out her flashlight and clicked it on. A sign on the wall said *Trader Joe's Gives Back. This location donated $804,000 of nearly expired food to local charities.* Who the hell wanted nearly expired food? Should have given them proper food, Trader Joe. Howard was too fat to get through, so he was trying to unjam the doors instead of taking off his pack. She moved through the checkouts and down the nearest aisle. He called after her, and Gloria made a note to give him shit for breaking the Golden Rule. No Loud Noises!

The only time she had seen the infected on TV was shaky footage on the Nightly News. Lester Holt said they were sick, but Gloria just thought they were scary. They were probably all dead, but who knew? Maybe they were hiding out in places like Trader Joe's. Gloria shuddered, and moved through the store more carefully, shining her light into the shadows. But there was no one, infected, dead, or otherwise. After a few more minutes, she gave up looking and searched instead for sunglasses. There they were, between the sunscreen and fake tan. Sunglasses! Bless you, Trader Joe!

There was only one kind, like the ones Jon Hamm wore in Mad Men, polarized with a shiny metal frame. Not bad for $12 and even better for free. She always had a thing for Jon Hamm. Gloria wondered where he was now. She took two pairs. What the hell, she could afford it. Howard was calling for her again, off in another part of the store. Bigmouth. Gloria had what she wanted so she went back to the doors. There was nothing here they couldn't get in Safeway. It was brighter near the open door, so she slid the flashlight into her pocket. While she waited for Howard, she stared at her reflection in the glass.

"There you are," said Howard. "There's a washroom at the back."

He wandered over with a full shopping bag. Gloria pointed at her sunglasses.

"Oh," he said. "Nice."

Not much of a compliment. Howard's fawning annoyed her, but not fawning annoyed her more. Gloria was aware this said more about her psyche than his, but there were no psychologists anymore, so the apocalypse wasn't all bad.

"What's with all the stuff?" she asked.

"Things we might need."

"You can get all this shit in Safeway."

"Safeway won't last forever."

"You'll be carrying it for miles, Howard."

He shrugged. "I'll put it in my pack, it's not heavy."

"I'm going to the washroom."

She stalked off through the store. Gloria opened the door and inspected the facilities. Relatively clean. After peeing, she wiped the mirror on the wall. With the red hood, glasses, and scarf, she was like some sort of Christmas bandit. Gloria took it all off and rubbed life into her skin. Cold aged her.

"Who's going to think you're 32 now?"

Howard was already outside when she got back, eating a bag of candy-covered peanuts. They shared them as they went back along the street.

"What happened to Hollywood?" asked Gloria.

"The place?"

"The people. The movie stars."

"Probably dead."

"Why would they be dead?"

"They wouldn't have the skills, wouldn't know how to survive."

"You were a bookkeeper, Howard."

"That's different. I was prepared."

She rolled her eyes. As they reached Pennsylvania Avenue, Gloria turned and called back.

"So long, Trader Joe!"

"Glory!" hissed Howard. "The Golden Rule!"

"You were shouting your head off in the store."

"It was empty."

"You're full of crap."

They headed off again, between the cars.

"Who were you talking to, anyway?" asked Howard.

"Trader Joe."

"The store?"

"The man. The real Trader Joe, if there is a Trader Joe."

"There is. Or was. He's dead."

"Everyone's dead, Howard."

Gloria could see Washington Circle ahead, clogged with traffic around the park. They tried to skirt the perimeter to avoid the press of vehicles, but a DC Circulator had come off the road and hit a wall near the George Washington University Hospital. There didn't seem to be any way passed the bus, so Gloria threaded through the cars and cut across the park. The snow was thicker here, but there was no other impediment. It seemed more open than before, trees wind-blasted, some toppled, the grass entirely covered in a thick layer of white, like cream. She missed cream. Fresh cream, poured on chewy pavlova. Wooden benches poked out at regular intervals around the curving path. There was a figure sitting on one of them with a frost-thick blanket over its head. She looked away and dreamed of dessert.

The statue of Washington was ahead, on his horse, dressed like a general, sword drawn. She saluted.

"Look what they did to your city, George."

"What?" called Howard.

She waved to him and went on, picking through the mash of cars at the other end. Gloria caught a whiff of something wrong. Something rotten. If she could smell it in the wind with a scarf over her face, it must be pretty rank. The infected. She wrapped her hand around the crossbow in its holster. This was it, they were going to see the infected face-to-face. Gloria drew the weapon and pulled back the charging handle. The bowstring tensed and locked into place with a tiny click.

"Howard," she called in one of those stage whispers.

He made his way over to her. "Are you OK?"

"Keep your voice down. The air stinks."

He rapped his respirator. "I can't smell anything."

"That's why I'm telling you."

"Is it them?"

"It's got to be."

Howard raised his crossbow and Gloria slapped it away.

"Aim that thing somewhere else."

Pulling her scarf down, she sniffed the air. Vile. Gloria spat and went to the back of a silver Ford Expedition to peek around. Ten yards away was a refrigerated Metro Poultry truck hemmed in by cars. A pickup had crashed into the back and the seals were broken. The sour taint wafted out on the wind.

"What is it?" he asked, crossbow rising.

"Just meat."

"Meat?"

"Rotting meat, in the back of a truck."

Gloria didn't understand why meat would stink so bad when the city was a freezer, but she didn't care. They headed off through the maze of cars, Howard to her rear, aiming his weapon at possible threats in a series of nervous jerks. Gloria told him to stop it and he put the weapon away. Before long, they were back on the main sprawl of the Avenue and they trudged on in silence for what seemed like an age.

"You think other countries are left?" asked Gloria.

"What countries?"

"You know, Canada, England."

"No."

Gloria felt her irritation rise. "Why not?"

"Canada's got a long border, they couldn't stop that many infected coming from the States."

"How many?"

"Millions."

She couldn't even imagine so many.

"What about England?"

"Britain's an island, but London's like New York, people fly in from everywhere every day. All it takes is one bite."

"OK, no more."

"I was just telling you."

"Do you always have to tell me everything? Can't you just lie?"

Howard stopped abruptly, staring ahead. Farther down the street was a line of bulky vehicles parked end to end across the road. Howard whistled.

"They're tanks."

"I know that, Howard."

She started forward and he grabbed her arm. "What are you doing?"

"Checking it out."

"But there might be soldiers."

Gloria shook his hand off and started toward the roadblock, leaving Howard where he was. Of course, there might be soldiers, that was the point. Soldiers meant rescue. Her idea of heaven wasn't living in an RV with Howard staring at her ass. As she came closer to the nearest tank, Gloria was struck by how big it was. 30 feet from end to end, the main gun could take out a city block. The tank didn't need weapons to kill the infected, it could roll over them. It was unbeatable. Her heart sank as she saw packed snow around the tracks. It hadn't moved in months.

Walking forward she touched the armored flank. Invincible. She grabbed a metal handhold and heaved herself up. Dozens of tanks ran right along H Street, cordoning off Lafayette Square. Then she saw a soldier. He was hanging out of a hatch on the next tank, frozen to the metal. His helmet was strange, smooth like a football player with big earphones. Gloria was close enough to see broken ribs sticking through his uniform and bite marks. Why didn't you stay in the tank? They couldn't get you if you stayed in the tank.

"They were guarding the White House," said Howard. He was standing in the snow below.

"Can you see it?"

"No," she said, "I don't want to see it and I don't want you to, either."

"Why not?"

"Because I don't."

She climbed down the other side. From the ground, the line of tanks along H Street obscured Pennsylvania Avenue, and her anxiety eased a little. Gloria's emotions roiled inside her. There was only so much end of the world she could take. She pushed on through the snow. The procession of war machines seemed endless. How had they lost? For the life of her, she did not understand how sick people, even a million sick people, could beat a tank. They weren't even damaged. It took a few minutes to notice Howard wasn't with her. Gloria turned to see him farther back, standing on one of the tanks. He was staring toward the White House.

She couldn't believe it. Gloria had specifically asked him not to, but he was doing it anyway. Angrily, she tramped off along H Street until she came to another roadblock, letting the rage smolder as she looked at the corpses. A body was nearby, close enough to touch. It was slumped in the cab of a truck, helmeted head on the wheel like a drunk. She didn't flinch. Cold blurred the edges, making him less human, like a waxwork. She heard Howard catching up to her.

"Go back," she said.

"What?"

"I'm going by myself."

"Glory?"

"You don't give a shit about anyone else, do you?"

Howard blinked. "What do you mean?"

"I mean I told you not to look, but you did it anyway."

"I just wanted to see."

"And I wanted not to know, but you couldn't even let me have that."

"Glory…"

"Why did you save me just to make my life a misery?" Her voice was getting louder. "Everyone's dead except you. Do you know what it's like to have to wake up every day and look at your face? Do you know what that's like? Do you have any idea?"

"I didn't tell you anything."

"Of course, you told me, you can't help yourself, it's written all over your rat face. It's all over you, you stink of it."

Before Howard could reply, Gloria marched off. She climbed up the nearest tank while Howard was still thinking of something to say. Holding on to the side of the turret to steady herself, she looked along H Street to the Women's Art Museum. The spire of the Presbyterian Church rose high above the surrounding buildings, glinting in the morning light. It was beautiful in the way deserts are beautiful. She calmed a little. The way ahead was clearer, only a few cars. Gloria dropped down on the other side, adjusted her pack, and set off at a pace Howard would strain to match. Serve him right if his heart burst like a balloon.

He managed to catch up to her, huffing and puffing, but it did him no good. She was done talking. Howard tried his best over the next 20 minutes, but Gloria didn't say a word. He stopped trying to apologize, following on like a naughty boy behind his mom. Half an hour later they passed the Metro Center. Almost there.

"I'm sorry, Glory," said Howard.

"You're not sorry, you're not sorry at all."

"I just wanted to see. I thought if I had a quick look it would be OK."

She didn't reply and kept on walking.

"It was burned. They burned it."

Gloria turned on the man. "Why the fuck would you tell me that? I told you I didn't want to know!"

"You said you knew anyway."

"How could I know?"

"You said I stink of it."

"For fuck sake!" she shouted. "You're pathetic!"

Gloria spun around and walked past the Capitol City Brewing Company on the corner. Arc'teryx was across the street. It was in a sorry state, the first-floor windows smashed.

Howard walked towards her.

"Glory…"

"I don't want to hear it, Howard! Go back to Dorothy! You can jerk off till you're blue in the face."

"Don't be like that, Glory."

"Stop calling me that!" she screamed.

Every bit of frustration that built up over the months cooped up with Howard in the RV came spilling out. She had passed the point of no return and she was never going back.

"Gloria! My fucking name is Gloria!"

Her voice was echoing off the buildings all around them.

"I told you a million fucking times, that's not my fucking name! But it doesn't matter anymore. You know why? Because I never want to see your fat fucking face ever again!"

Overwhelmed with rage, Gloria stormed across the road towards Arc'teryx. She wouldn't look back, she wouldn't pity him, and she wouldn't put up with him anymore and never go back to Dorothy. She would rather starve. When she was halfway across 11th Street, she heard something, like rushing water. She turned to see hundreds of people pouring out of buildings farther down the street. The rushing sound was their feet in the snow. Men, women, and children merged into a mass that filled the roadway. It took Gloria a second before she realized what she was seeing.

They were infected. Terror gripped her as they surged forward. She ran, as fast as she could in the deep snow, pushing across to Arc'teryx on the other side. It was her only hope. Gloria tried not to look at the mass as they charged. Some of them were children. Children! Blank eyes and bared teeth, skin like unburied bodies. This was all her fault. Shouting at Howard like a harpy and breaking the Golden Rule. She was going to be ripped apart by the people she had cheated by staying alive. This was their revenge.

She finally made it to the far side and looked for a way into the store as the infected bore down on her. They were howling now and the sound was terrifying. Crawling through a broken window, Gloria found herself in the dim interior with nowhere to hide. She ran along the aisles to the stairs at the back, heart beating like a drum. They were right behind her, ready to pull her down and rip her apart. She could feel the teeth in her skin, nails scratching her face. She took the steps three at a time. On the second floor, she turned this way and that, desperate to find somewhere safe.

The gunshot was crisp and clear. For a moment, Gloria wondered who it could be, then she remembered. Howard. Howard was still out there. Knocking over a mannequin, she ran to the window. Below, the tide of infected milled around in confusion. They had lost sight of her and then heard the shot, they didn't know which way to go. Howard stood across the street holding the pistol, aimed up like the start of a race. He fired again. The mass of infected rippled as they turned to face the sound and streamed toward the lone figure in orange. Gloria couldn't look but she couldn't look away. Howard lowered the gun as the mass enveloped him.

She stumbled back into the darkness and felt her way along the wall. Gloria found a door and opened it. Inside was black and smelled of cigarettes. She slammed it closed and slid down, her back against the wood. All she could think of was Howard. Something moved outside, chuffing near the door. Part of her wanted to open it, to end it all. But a greater part wanted to live. Memories of Howard tore at her. The police car, the gun. *You can use it to protect me. Be my guardian angel.* The terrible things she said. Howard on his own across the street, the infected sweeping over him. Tears ran down her face as she held the door closed, her heart breaking for a man she had never loved.

Chapter 10

The image blurred before focusing on the man below. *Larry's Repair* was stenciled across his coveralls, a mechanic, maybe even Larry himself. If it was, Larry was having a bad day. From this height, Gath had a clear view of the back of Union Station through the falling snow. There were hundreds of people milling around down there, like rush hour. He was infected, but then they were all infected. Eyes the same foggy white, skin like parchment pulled too tight across the skull. Larry was looking up, a strange expression on his face. It seemed like grief, but it couldn't be. Infected didn't have emotions, that part of the brain had rotted away. Larry's cheeks were wet, a liquid shine that had yet to freeze. Whether this was from tears or melting snow, it was impossible to say.

"See what I mean?" asked McCord.

They were in a maintenance alcove on the station roof. It was the highest place in the complex they could get to. The two men crouched a few feet from a hatch that led back down to Operations. The curved roof of the Great Hall swept up another thirty feet behind, blocking the worst of the wind. Gath shivered, not just because of the cold. He wore an Amtrak police windbreaker over his hiking jacket. The bottom half of his flight suit was covered by baggy maintenance pants. McCord had his riot gear, which he maintained was as good against the weather as it was against teeth.

"I'm not sayin' I told you so, Colonel, but I did tell you so."

He had to raise his voice over the wind. Gath didn't reply and panned his binoculars to the high-rise car lot on the left. It rose a couple of stories above their vantage point. The level opposite was empty except for a Toyota pickup. It had hit the safety barrier, breaking a hole in the railing. The front wheels hung out over empty space. A sudden gust whipsawed across the concrete, sending snow and trash twirling like tumbleweed. Gath looked down again. The platforms were covered by a flat roof against the rain, with the tracks running out to the H Street Overpass for trains to come and go. Infected were everywhere.

Gath lowered the binoculars and spat into the wind. He had hoped for a surgical strike to restart the generators, but there were just too many. Movement in the car lot caught his eye. A woman in a yellow raincoat lurched around the pickup and fell through the break in the barrier. She dropped into the infected below. The crowd didn't react and kept shambling along, following some instinct to keep on moving. He saw yellow again and the woman was up, merging with the rest like nothing had happened.

"Part of your perimeter's down," said Gath, pointing. "That's how they're getting in."

"It's down in a couple of places. No way to fix it. They come in along the tracks too. Some fall off the overpass, get right up again. Can't lock it all down."

Gath rubbed his eyes, work gloves rough against the skin. McCord leaned in and tapped the binoculars.

"NASA?"

"Walmart. I've seen enough. Let's get the hell out of Dodge before my balls freeze."

McCord shook his head. "There you go again."

The old policeman didn't like cursing and complained every time he heard it.

Gath held up a hand "If we're going to argue, dear, let's not do it in front of the children."

He moved to the hatch and they made their way down the ladder. It was a relief to be out of the stinging cold. The descent made Gath's legs come back to life as the blood remembered its job. They exited into a maintenance area.

"Must have been hard being a religious cop," said Gath.

"Bein' right ain't hard."

"Anyone else think you were right?"

"Only at the end."

Both men wiped the snow off their clothes as McCord flicked on his flashlight. They passed through long-term storage and the cafeteria. The older man took off his helmet and gas mask as they walked.

"Do you have faith, Colonel?"

"Riding 1400 tons of fuel into orbit needs a little faith."

"Didn't answer my question."

"I know."

When they were back in the locker room, McCord dumped his headgear.

"It's like I said, them things are everywhere."

Gath pulled down his hood and took off the windbreaker.

"Just needed the see the lay of the land."

"You'd need an army to get to the generators."

Gath walked into the Control Room. Charlie, Chen, and Nix were sitting together, wrapped in blankets, listening to country music. A pile of batteries lay beside the old CD player. Chen stood up and offered her blanket to Gath who smiled. It was still warm. He dried himself off a little, then rubbed his legs back to life. Charlie turned off the music.

"Anywhere in the station we can get more outdoor clothes?" she asked Nix.

"I've been through the stores, it's mostly fashion. All the heavy stuff's gone from H&M. The only warm things are police and maintenance gear, but there's not enough."

McCord stripped off his armor. "It was gettin' cold when the station shut. People took the warm stuff."

"What about the lockers?" asked Charlie. "People leave clothes in their lockers all the time."

"Don't have keys."

"Break them open."

McCord frowned. "That's private property."

"So are the stores you've been looting."

"Ain't the same."

"Why not?"

"We got keys to them places."

Gath cleared his throat. "I think we're beyond worrying about the law, Sarge."

"Them lockers belong to people. Friends of mine."

Charlie stood up. "I'm sorry Bill. Your friends aren't coming back."

When they finished opening the lockers, they put their haul in two small piles on the benches. Maintenance and construction gear, pants and gloves, custodial overalls, jackets of different types, and another police windbreaker. Though there were no shoes of any use, they did find a stash of Snickers bars. Nix played no part in the search, making coffee as an act of solidarity for the angry old man. When it was over, the five of them gathered around again in the Control Room. Gath searched through the papers in a rack below one of the security monitors as the others arranged themselves on chairs or the floor. McCord watched him, then let out a long, exasperated sigh.

"What are you after?"

Gath kept searching. "Pen and paper."

The old man got up and opened a drawer near Nix's chair, groped around, and then brought out a pad of paper and a pencil. Gath took them with a smile that wasn't returned, then sat on the floor with his back to the wall.

"Step One, we get the power back on. Step Two, we get cold weather gear."

"Which step is finding more food?" asked Charlie.

"That's Step Three. Once we get the power on, we can cook up stuff from the pizza place. We can live on that until we find snow gear, then hit the supermarkets."

"I know a place," said Nix.

"Where?"

"Outdoor clothing place, hiking, skiing."

"Near here?"

"Never walked from here. It's on H Street. Maybe a half-hour. At least it used to be. Probably a two or three-hour hike now."

"Why don't we just get food nearby," said McCord.

"As we empty stores, we'll have to go on longer and longer trips. Every time increases the risk of frostbite and hypothermia. My feet are halfway there. We need warm, waterproof clothes and hot food in our bellies."

Nix grinned. "I want goulash."

"I'll settle for coffee," said McCord.

He held out his mug. Nix collected all the empties, then went to the kitchen with Charlie.

"One little problem, Colonel," said McCord. "We ain't gettin' the power on."

Gath leaned forward and started sketching on the pad. McCord watched him for a while, then turned to Chen.

"Figure you've come a long way, Miss. Not seeing DC at its best."

Gath finished whatever he was drawing. Nix and Charlie came back with mugs and a plate of cut-up Snickers, passing them out. Gath beckoned everyone to join him on the floor.

"This is a map of the station."

"Looks like a couple of lines to me," said McCord.

"If I get anything wrong, let me know."

"You can bet on that, Colonel."

Gath began again. "There are hundreds of infected around the tracks and inside the perimeter fence. More than a thousand."

That dampened the enthusiasm brought on by the chocolate. Charlie bit into her Snickers.

"How did they get in?"

"Fence is down in places and they can access the complex along the tracks and from other structures."

"I don't understand," said Chen.

Gath held the pencil above the pad, then dropped it.

"I saw one fall 60 feet and get up again. Bill saw them do the same from the overpass. There are too many to shoot, even if we had enough ammo, which we don't. No way to stop it."

"Why are they here?" asked Charlie.

"They have to be somewhere."

"They could be anywhere. Why come here?" She turned to McCord. "When did you first notice infected on the tracks?"

"After the station closed. Late December."

"Was there any noise in the station after it closed?"

"Quiet as the grave. Made sure the place was secure, checked the generators, cleared the tracks."

Charlie put a hand on his arm. "Cleared them of what?"

"Them things. A few used to wander in, we could handle a few."

"How did you handle them?"

"Shot them."

"The generators were working?"

"Sure."

"So, you were running diesel generators and firing weapons?"

McCord looked confused.

"Nothing you could do," said Gath, "but the noise probably brought the infected. I guess when the generators went offline, they just stuck around."

"We did our duty," said the old man.

Nix licked his fingers. "We need to find more Snickers."

There was a murmur of agreement. Charlie leaned towards McCord.

"When were you and Nix asked to guard the station?"

"Kid came later."

"Maybe you could tell us what happened from the start, Bill. The more we know, the more we can help."

He was going to say no but she smiled her best smile. The policeman collected his thoughts.

"At the start, there were eight of us," said McCord, sipping from his mug. "Four cops and four maintenance. The station was essential infrastructure, they said. Had to be secure. They said a lot of things. Orders were to hold the station 'til relieved, so we locked all the doors and sealed the shutters. Hunkered down inside and waited for things to get better."

McCord ran a hand over his craggy chin.

"They got worse. We saw it all on the cameras. Never seen nothin' like it. People runnin' through the snow, soldiers shootin'. Bigger and bigger waves of them things washed them army boys away. There was a little girl, can't have been more than five years old, sittin' in her mamma's coat. Pulled her apart like a chicken wing."

The old policeman took a long sip of coffee. His hands were shaking.

"Maintenance guys lit out first, took the truck. Ford and Ramirez went next, headed on foot to the 14th Street Bridge to make a run for Arlington. They had families. Was just me and George left."

"George?" asked Gath.

"George Honneker. Veteran, like me."

"What happened to him?"

McCord said nothing, but he didn't need to. It was a stupid question. The old man blinked a few times and ran a hand over his gray stubble.

"Things got quiet when the big storm hit. Buried the city. No one could survive in that. Ford said he'd get a message to us on the radio when he was safe, but there was nothing. I figure George and me were the lucky ones."

McCord took a sip of coffee, swirled it around his mouth, and then wiped his lips. The drink was his prop, giving him time to get things straight. He took another sip.

"Went from bad to worse. More of them things turned up on the tracks. We had to clear them out to keep the generators runnin' and get to the heavy equipment store. But they kept comin'. Used service weapons 'til we ran out of ammo, then switched to the Mossberg. A shotgun on sick people. Hell of a thing."

McCord's eyes were unfocused like he was looking at something only he could see. Gath had seen the look before. The thousand-yard stare. Something was loose in there, rattling around. Post-traumatic stress disorder. Gath supposed it didn't matter. Just being alive these days was PTSD. McCord reached out and grabbed Gath's forearm, fingers digging in.

"You ever seen what double-ought buckshot does to a head?"

Gath looked into the old man's eyes. He was scared, wouldn't take much to push him over the edge. They stared at each other for a few heartbeats, then McCord released his grip.

"Gettin' their blood off the concrete's the hard part. Sticky. Like molasses. When the shells ran out, we chained the doors. First time the generators stopped was a week later. Me and George fought our way out with the Milkors, but they was pretty much useless. We didn't try to reload, just used them like clubs. Only the Lord and riot gear got us back in one piece. Next time the generators stopped, they stopped for good. There were too many of them things and George was gone."

"When happened to him?"

McCord's face hardened. "Days were slow. Not much to do but listen to the radio and watch the cameras. George spotted a couple of folks runnin' hell for leather for the West Entrance. We high-tailed it, no time for riot gear. When we got the shutters up, two fellas was makin' a beeline for us, a dozen of them things hot on their heels. First fella runs in and I grab him, check him for bites. Other one falls. George runs out, no weapon, no armor, but he runs out anyway. That's what George was like. By the time I got to the door, them things were all over him. Snow was red. I closed the shutters."

Nix looked like a dog who had been kicked. No prizes for guessing he was the one who was saved.

"Power will give us heating, hot showers, proper food, and security systems. We could even set up a basic clinic. We just won't survive without power. But there's too many infected to fight."

McCord nodded. "Like I said."

"So we won't fight. We'll create a diversion, clear the platforms long enough to get the generators running. We'll rig your loudhailer up to the CD player, leave it playing 500 yards outside the eastern fence line. Once the infected leave, we'll go out and fix the generators."

"Won't work," said McCord.

"Why not?"

"Could take hours to fix."

"How long did it take last time?"

"That was different, they just needed a reset. They've been off for weeks, could be froze solid. Three of them daisy-chained together. When one stops, the next one's supposed to kick in, but it didn't. Could be all three of them's busted."

"Chen's a mechanical engineer. We'll get them running."

"Thought she was a pilot?"

"She's a pilot too."

"It still won't work."

"Why not?"

"500 yards is too far away. They'll never hear it with the wind."

"Then we'll bring it closer. 100 yards outside the fence," said Gath, scribbling on the paper. "We don't want it too close or they might get there, see there's nothing to eat then come back. What else?"

McCord tapped the paper. "That part of the fence is down. They'll see nobody's there."

"I don't think they can see," said Nix.

"You an eye doctor now?"

The boy flushed. "One walked right past me when we were looking for food. I just stood there, too scared to move. It left me alone."

"That's not proof."

"We don't need proof," said Gath. "Noise brought them to the generators and nobody's there either. All we need is enough time to get them working. How long does it take to reset, Sarge?"

"Five minutes. Maybe more, maybe less. But if they're froze, your goose is cooked."

"Are they sheltered from the wind?"

McCord didn't see the connection. "They're in big metal cabinets in the middle of Track 6. There's a roof, but it's open to the cold."

"What's the fuel capacity?"

"300 gallons each."

"Diesel gets cloudy in the extreme cold and turns to jelly as the paraffin starts to crystallize. But it's a long process. 300 gallons in shelter should be fine. I'm not worried."

"That makes one of us."

"Anything else?"

"We need a cover for the CD player," said Chen. "The snow can stop it from working."

"Good, we'll find one," Gath made a note. "What else?"

Charlie chewed her lip. "How will we know when the infected leave? I mean, we don't know how long it takes for them to hear music and go have a look."

Gath thought then made a note on the paper. "We'll just have to guess. As soon as we hear the music, we'll give them five minutes to get clear then open the doors."

McCord shook his head. "If we get the generators on, they'll hear the noise and come back."

"We'll be gone by then."

The old cop snorted.

"We've nothing to lose," said Gath.

"Unless one of us gets bit. Even if we do get them workin', what do we do when they stop again?"

"If we're still alive, I'll let you know. What else?"

"Who's going out with the loudhailer?" asked Charlie.

"Nix. I need the Sarge for the generators. Me, you, and Chen will cover him while he works."

"We can't send Nix out there on his own."

The young man's eyes widened. "I'll be fine."

"We're not sending him out alone. You know what happened last time."

"Neet wasn't alone," said Gath.

"She died anyway."

"Someone who knows the place needs to do it and I need Bill with me."

"Then I'm going with him."

Gath stared at her. "I need as many shooters as possible, in case we get into trouble."

"What about Nix? You don't know what's out there."

"The infected are at the generators."

"All of them? Do you know that for sure? We're not sending the boy out there by himself."

"I'm not a boy," said Nix.

Charlie ignored him. "Give Bill a gun, you'll still have three shooters. If you wait 10 minutes before you open the doors, I should be able to get back. Then you'll have four. That's a good deal, so no point arguing."

Gath didn't like it but there wasn't much he could do. He smiled.

"Then I won't argue."

The young man's blush could fry an egg. Gath made another notation on the paper.

"Charlie and Nix will place the diversion and then come back. The whole thing will be a matter of timing." He stood up. "We'll need tools, tape, and something to wrap the CD player. Give Bill the Sig."

Chen reached into a sports bag and took out a holstered weapon, a 9mm Sig Sauer. Neet's weapon. Chen handed it to McCord.

"There are only eight rounds left in the magazine," said Gath. "If we can get away without firing a shot, we will. We don't want to ring the dinner bell. How hard is it to find ammunition in DC?"

"No way on God's clean Earth," said the old cop. "Blame the Democrats."

Chapter 11

"Hey, Doc, it's me."

The man held Prashad close, to stop her from doing anything else stupid. He smelled of blood and rot but she sagged into his arms anyway. Relief washed over her. One minute she was going to die, the next she wasn't. Prashad held on with no intention of letting go. She knew the voice but couldn't remember his name.

"Corporal Mapuya," he said, reading her mind. "When I let go, try not to shoot me."

As his hands released, Prashad continued to grip the soldier's parka. She wasn't ready to be on her own.

"It's alright, Doc," said Mapuya.

Another light clicked on, dust drifting through the beam. Prashad saw the outline of a helmet. He held a submachine gun with another slung over his shoulder. His camouflage gear was grimy and spattered with gore.

"What's your name again?"

"Mapuya. Everyone calls me Maps."

"You've got a lot of guns, Maps."

"I need a lot."

"Why are you still here?"

"Looking for you."

"I hid in the labs."

"I checked the labs."

"In a cabinet."

"Smart." He panned his weapon light around the room. "Think we're OK for now."

"What about the infected?"

"Got most of them."

"I got two."

He turned back. "You scratched or bitten?"

"Scratches don't transmit the pathogen."

"Did you get scratched?"

"No. Nothing. Bites infect because their gums bleed," Prashad went on, not sure why she kept talking. "The disease is bloodborne. Transmits when teeth break the skin."

"If you say so, Doc. How's your ammo?"

"I've got two magazines and what's in the gun."

Mapuya handed her two more. "Spares. How many shots did you fire?"

"I don't know."

"Change the mag and keep the one you've fired in a different pouch. That's your backup when you've run out."

"You think we'll run out?"

"Learn to count, it could save your life. You know how to reload?"

Prashad nodded and released the magazine. It fell onto the floor and she bent to look for it, feeling foolish. It took half a minute more to find the magazine, load the weapon, and put the spares in her pouch. The Corporal watched her without speaking.

"Ready?" he asked.

She nodded, glad he couldn't see her blush. The wind was picking up outside, blowing eddies through the window. Mapuya waved her to follow him out into the corridor. It was pitch black.

"Sorry I was hiding when you came looking for me," she said.

"You were right to hide, Doc, I hid too."

"But you killed them."

"One by one. Rest of the time, I hid."

Mapuya checked both ends of the corridor. Prashad saw the soft glow of the Merson. Copeland's weapon.

"See anything?"

"Nah. If the damn thing even works."

"Where's the Sergeant?"

The man paused before answering. "He didn't make it."

"I know he didn't make it, Maps. Where's the body?"

"Outside. He'll keep in the cold until we can get a recovery team." Mapuya turned to face her. "Sarge told me what happened on comms. Why'd Lang do it?"

"No idea."

Prashad wasn't going to share what she knew. Everyone had an agenda at Aegis.

"Sex," said the Corporal.

"What?"

"It was sex. You've got to have a reason to shoot somebody, always sex or money. There's no money anymore, so it's got to be sex."

What nonsense. "Did you find her body?"

"Nah. She got away or she's a Munchie."

"Munchie?"

"Infected," said Mapuya. "You know, munch munch."

"If she's infected, we need to shoot her and see what she's carrying. She might have something we need."

"I'm shooting her anyway, Doc, she's got it coming."

Prashad didn't argue. "Why are we standing in the corridor?"

"It's warmer."

"Why don't we just go?"

"Go where?"

"Back to the transport."

"Matvee's gone. Erlich was on comms when the shooting started, but I was otherwise occupied. I couldn't raise her. She's either dead or RTB."

RTB meant Return to Base.

"She would reply if she was home," said Prashad.

"Unit comms only run a couple of miles. Regs say after losing radio contact, try to reestablish communications without endangering the mission. If not, RTB."

"So, she's home."

"Erlich wouldn't just leave."

"You said regulations mean she has to go back."

"We don't leave our people."

Prashad nodded. "So what do we do? Call the QRF?"

"Need the Matvee's radio."

"So how do we find it?"

"Follow the tire tracks. Matvee weighs a shit ton, easy to see."

Prashad didn't like the thought of trekking through the snow, but there was no alternative. Mapuya slipped the other weapon from his shoulder.

"You want an SMG?"

SMG stood for submachine gun. The scientist shook her head and Mapuya tossed the extra weapon onto the floor. He pointed to the Merson.

"You know how this works?"

"I was briefed."

"It's an echolocator that can filter out large organic movements from background noise."

"Like I said, I was briefed."

"Lot of ghosts and false positives, but it's good and picking up Friend or Foe chips and the Matvee's transponder. As long as we're close enough. We'll find her."

"People say it's unreliable."

"People say I'm unreliable too," said Mapuya, "Don't listen to what people say."

"Don't let me down, Maps."

"No worries, I've got you." He took out a ration bar. "Hungry?"

"No."

"If we're walking, we'll need to keep it tight. When I say 'down', get down, turn your flashlight off. Noise discipline. Not a peep."

Prashad nodded. "Which way?"

"Through the building to the front doors then back to the road."

"There'll be more of those things."

"I guess so."

"Lang went out of the window. Can't we go that way?"

"Could do, but I've no idea what's out there. Could be Munchies and nowhere to hide."

"It's night, maybe they won't see us. I need to get out of this place, Maps."

He nodded. "I hear you. Let's do it."

They went back through the broken doors. The wind had died down but Prashad felt the temperature drop despite the heating system in her snow camouflage.

"You can holster your weapon," said Mapuya.

"What if I need it?"

"When you need it, take it out. Just wandering about in the snow, though, it might go off."

"You said it only goes off when you pull the trigger."

"Look at your weapon."

"What about it?"

"Where's your finger?"

It was resting on the trigger. "Oh."

Prashad holstered it but kept the clip off. She hefted her flashlight as they moved to the window and climbed out, avoiding glass along the edges. Outside, they stood at the top of a small hill, lights searching. University buildings seemed to press too close at night. Copeland's body was nearby, helmet over his face. Prashad never liked the man. Mapuya aimed his weapon light down the slope and then started walking. She followed until he stopped at the bottom and crouched, examining the ground.

"Single set of boot prints, going west."

"We're going west."

Mapuya didn't say anything to that.

"Infected?" asked Prashad.

"Nah. Infected walk like drunks."

"You sound like you've done this before."

"This is my sixth trip."

Prashad didn't know there had been other missions into the city.

"Is it Lang?" she asked.

Mapuya nodded slowly. They went west, negotiating the snow as best they could. Prashad trod in the Corporal's footprints, which made it easier. It wasn't long before they turned north. The wind picked up and beat at them.

"Down!" hissed Mapuya.

They crouched and turned off the lights. Prashad could see a group of red dots on the Corporal's Merson. Fear touched her. She wanted to run but knew that meant death. Forcing herself to be still, she closed her eyes and waited. After what seemed like an age, Mapuya turned on his light and started off again. This was scary. They couldn't afford to make a mistake when the stakes were everything. Passing the front of the Medical Building, Mapuya crossed the road and stood at the steps that stretched down to the road. Their lights didn't reach far enough to see it, which was fine by Prashad. She didn't want to see that the M-ATV was really gone.

Mapuya turned to say something and he slipped, disappearing with a grunt. Prashad scrambled down the steps after him, going as fast as she could. Her light found him on the bottom step, weapon gone, trying to stand. He had fallen on a corpse, splayed out in the snow. Prashad used her free hand to help him up.

"Fuck," said Mapuya, wiping the front of his parka. "I smell like shit."

"You smelled like shit anyway."

There were more dead scattered around them. Infected. The Corporal nudged the body he had fallen on with his boot.

"Bagged by Erlich. PIKE rounds."

Prashad stepped over the dead and made her way toward the road. Her light found only tire tracks.

"Fuck."

Mapuya appeared beside her. He had found his weapon and was scanning the area. There were many more bodies bunched here and there in the snow.

"Erlich was out of the vehicle when they hit her," he said. "Probably coming to find us but she was forced back."

Mapuya bent to examine a woman's body in a blue dress. Her head had been crushed, leaking something like tar.

"Run over."

"How do you know?"

"No bullet holes."

Prashad blinked. She should have noticed, but she hadn't.

"Explains a lot," said the Corporal.

He walked to the tracks.

"What does it explain?" asked Prashad.

Mapuya stood and shone his light along the road, first one way and then the other.

"Explains why she left, why she was out of range when I got on comms."

"Doesn't explain why she didn't come back."

The Corporal said nothing.

"So what do we do now?"

Mapuya pointed. "Follow the tracks."

"She'll be back at Aegis by now."

"Nah. Erlich wouldn't leave."

"She would if she thought we were dead."

"She would check."

"How do you know?"

The Corporal headed off along the tracks. "It's what I would do."

"We can't walk with those things out there."

He kept on going, his light bobbing ahead. "You can stay, Doc, I'm going to find Erlich."

Prashad cursed and then hurried after him, along the great furrows in the snow. Neither spoke as they cut through a little thoroughfare and exited on a wider road. There were bodies here and there. Mapuya turned west for a while before stopping.

"We need a better plan," said Prashad.

The Corporal crouched by some tracks. "We could stay and make babies. Repopulate the human race." He stood. "Look, Doc, we either find Erlich or we walk home, it's that simple."

"Nothing's that simple."

"Out here, simple keeps you alive. C'mon."

He head off to the east and she trailed behind. A hundred yards or so farther up the road they saw more of the dead. Navigating outside by flashlight was scarier than she thought. Anything could come at them. Mapuya pointed at one of the bodies with a fist-sized hole in its back.

"She's using the 50."

He held up a large, spent bullet casing.

"Is that bad?"

"Too loud, brings the Munchies."

"Doesn't she know that?"

"She knows."

They moved on, passing more and more chewed-up bodies, so many they were forced to leave the tracks and skirt around to find somewhere they could walk. There were so many it stank, even in the wind.

"Heaven's a girl with a big gun," said Mapuya.

"She's got an armored transport and the gun. What have we got?"

He slapped her on the shoulder. "You've got me, Doc!"

The tracks led off the road to a snowbound embankment that dropped away into nothing.

"I'm not going down there," said Prashad.

"That's where the tracks are."

"You're going to get me killed."

"Watch yourself on the Slip 'n Slide."

Mapuya hurtled down the slope but Prashad went more carefully. She slipped halfway and rolled to the bottom. The Corporal lifted her to her feet, wiped off the snow, and they continued on. Prashad's world shrank to the beam of a flashlight. Suddenly, Mapuya grabbed her and pulled her down. They turned off their lights and waited. Prashad heard footsteps in the snow, lots of them. Her breathing seemed too loud and she started to pray for the first time since she was a kid. The torment ended when Mapuya's light came on and he helped her up.

"Sorry, no warning."

"How many?"

"Too many."

They went on. The close call had spooked them both and they traveled in silence. Prashad was left to her own thoughts for longer than she was comfortable. She dwelled on what could happen to them. After another half-hour, she started to flag. The deep snow was exhausting. Prashad yanked on Mapuya's sleeve and he got the message. Leaning against a lonely-looking tree, she caught her breath and pulled out her canteen.

"Don't you get tired?" she asked.

"I'm used to it."

The Corporal handed her two ration bars. "Keep one for later."

"I'm not hungry."

"Eat it. You need the calories."

Prashad lifted her mask to take a sip of water and then bit into the ration bar. When she felt up to it, she nodded and they moved on. The tracks led off the road. No slope this time, but Mapuya's light found a hole in a row of tall hedges. They came to a heavy corrugated iron gate, battered open. The snow was heavily trampled

"That's a lot of feet," said Prashad.

"We need to keep going."

"There are hundreds of them."

"Erlich might need help."

"Who's going to help us?"

Mapuya followed the tracks off into the night, his light flickering across the snow. Prashad had a strange feeling, like she was being watched. She shone her flashlight in a slow circle. There were some brick buildings near the gate and some trees. No one was there but the feeling remained. Mapuya returned.

"Army Field Hospital, down the lane, set up in a sports field. Looks deserted."

Prashad didn't say anything.

"You coming, Doc?"

She nodded and followed him through the gates. After a hundred yards, they came to lines of interlocking fencing that ran off into the night. Beyond the wire were rows of big military tents. Pennants hung from a taller brick building off to their right, too far away to read. There was no entrance, but the M-ATV had crushed a section of chain link so there wasn't any trouble getting through. The beam of Prashad's flashlight rested on a green and white sign hanging down from a roll of razor wire. *White's Disease. Symptoms? Report to Medical Administration A2. Shivers, Headaches, Muscle Pain, Skin Lesions.* She took another step to read the smaller print at the bottom. *Bitten? Report to Quarantine F1 immediately.*

They approached the side of a long tent. More stretched away into the dark. Mapuya walked to the corner and shone his weapon light.

"This place is a ghost town."

She shivered a little and stuck close to the Corporal as he followed the tracks of the M-ATV farther into the camp. She passed a flap blowing in the wind and peeked inside. The tent floor was covered in trash. An MRE wrapper blew against her boot, and she kicked it away. Meals Ready to Eat were standard military rations used in the field and for emergencies. They were pre-cooked, self-heating, and nutritious. Prashad thought they tasted like plastic. She aimed her flashlight along the tents but couldn't see inside. Perhaps this tent was a garbage dump, or maybe they were all like this.

Temporary military hospitals had been set up across Washington to fight White's Disease. Prashad hadn't heard of one near Georgetown, but it was hardly surprising. Lots of open spaces were being commandeered in the final days. For many people, this was the end of the road. There were even rumors of aid stations being set up to euthanize the infected. One camp healed the sick, the other camp killed them. How did doctors live with that? The answer was they didn't. When DC fell, they must have known it was judgment day.

Mapuya stood by a tent squashed into the snow.

"We should get out of here," said Prashad.

The Corporal didn't reply.

"Say something."

"The sooner we find Erlich, the sooner we go home."

"Let's go back to the road. We can walk back to Aegis. I'm scared, Maps."

Her voice was soft, like a little girl's. Mapuya laid a hand on her shoulder.

"We're close. In a few minutes, we'll be in the Matvee, and this'll just be a story."

He walked on. Prashad's insides twisted into a knot, but she followed. She didn't want to, but it was better than being alone. The Matvee's trail twisted like the driver was drunk. They came to an open area dotted with basins and clothes. Part of a tent's vinyl covering had been shorn away exposing what must be barracks, with lines of bunk beds and footlockers. More trash covered the ground. Mapuya's weapon light stopped its constant sweep and trained on a solid sheet metal fence 20 yards away. One side of the fencing was down, crushed flat by the M-ATV sticking out of it. The vehicle was pitched forward like the front was sinking, the back wheels a foot in the air.

"Bingo," said the Corporal.

He stayed where he was, watching the Merson.

"She's still in there."

"That's good, isn't it?" asked Prashad.

The Corporal touched the push-to-talk button on his helmet comm.

"Headhunter 3, Headhunter 3, this is Headhunter 2. Over."

He waited for a response but there was nothing.

"C'mon, girl."

He repeated the hail but there was still no response. Mapuya started forward but Prashad grabbed him.

"What?" he asked.

"There's something wrong."

"If she's hurt, we're going to need you, Doc."

"I'm not that kind of doctor."

"You're close enough."

Mapuya walked towards the vehicle. She didn't argue, he wouldn't stop now. Following with small steps, her light joined his on the rear hatches. Blood and less identifiable organic matter were smeared across the paintwork. Mapuya moved to the passenger door but stopped. The vehicle wasn't sinking, it had driven into some sort of hole. A pit might be a better description, The door could only be opened by jumping down. Mapuya aimed his light and Prashad smelled the body bags before she saw them. The pit was full of them, the last few wrapped in bloody white sheets. She took a step closer and then jumped back.

"Someone's down there," she said, breathing too fast.

"Infected," said Mapuya, peering down.

Prashad spat in the snow and then took a swig from her canteen.

"Can they get out?"

"Nah."

Prashad joined Mapuya at the edge. There were four infected glaring up with fish-belly eyes. The faces were a bad dream. One of them tried to climb the plastic-covered side of the pit with no success. Another glared at Prashad, teeth gnashing.

"Like dogs," said Mapuya, "chased Erlich into the hole and couldn't get out."

Mapuya aimed and fired, blowing away a chunk of skull and dropping the nearest infected. It was a more difficult angle with the next, but he put three rounds through its side and it fell beside the first. He walked around M-ATV firing short, suppressed bursts.

"Driver's side is blocked. Have to use the passenger door." That meant climbing into the pit. He clipped his weapon to the front of his webbing to free his hands. "Shine your flashlight at the passenger door."

Prashad did as she was told, then swung away. Mapuya slowly unclipped his weapon.

"What is it?"

She ran her light along the tents. "Did you hear that?"

"What?"

Putting a finger to her lips, she drew her pistol. "I heard something."

"Merson says there's nothing there."

He stiffened and raised his weapon. "I hear it now."

Their lights tracked in the same direction, looking for whatever was out there.

"Like breathing," said Prashad.

Mapuya's head snapped up. "Got a contact, dead ahead, 30 yards."

Prashad froze. Something was there, something big, standing beyond the light. Its breathing was harsh and labored, like an animal. Then it roared.

Chapter 12

The tanker truck completely blocked the road. It had swerved, hit the outer wall of the Union Station complex, and flipped over. The cab was crumpled against brickwork on one side of the street, the back wheels wedged against a warehouse on the other. A ragged line of abandoned cars ran up to it with their doors open. Snow lay thick on everything. If the tanker had exploded, it would have been a disaster. Whether anyone would have noticed, in the middle of so many other disasters, was hard to say. But there was no explosion, and the moment was frozen in time. The crash, like the city wrapped around it, was just a memory now.

Charlie was on an access road that ran around the back of the station to the bus terminal. The wind had worsened and she hugged the maintenance coat around her. It would have kept the cold out completely if it wasn't eight sizes too big. She adjusted the pack and pulled her hood down. Most of her face was still exposed, but she would be back before anything dropped off. Nix was beside her, struggling in his riot gear. The gas mask meant she couldn't see his eyes and she missed them. He was so eager to be useful that he didn't consider the risk. Young people never worried about the future because there was so damned much of it.

Charlie looked through an open door and the backseat stuffed with suitcases and garbage bags. People had left everything behind to get away from the danger and they never came back. A bag had split and a little dinosaur stared at her. She couldn't remember what kind it was, but it was something someone couldn't live without. Triceratops. It was a triceratops. Charlie threaded her way through the cars. The tanker shouldn't have been on such a narrow road but there seemed to be no reason for the crash. A mystery, but stranger things had happened in the final days.

The driver's cab was on its side, one wheel above her head. Nix helped Charlie up and she held out a hand to return the favor. She climbed across the driver's door. *Petro Home Service*s was written underneath a cracked window. They jumped down to the other side. The rest of the road had no cars, only pristine snow. It was beautiful. Nix was breathing hard, the armor too heavy. He needed to toughen up. The gas mask made him look like a machine, but he wasn't a machine. He was a boy and boys could die.

She checked her watch. It was a Batman one for children she got from the gift stand. The battery was low, the digits faded under the Joker's laminated grin. 15 minutes to get to the outer fence and turn on the music, 10 minutes to get back. Straightforward. Charlie couldn't see any infected. If something went wrong, she had her pistol and Nix had the Milkor. The riot gun was too big to drag out here, but it gave Nix confidence. She reached down and unclipped the strap on her holster. Best to be prepared. The wind picked up as they approached the open gate, avoiding a half-buried body.

Beyond was a parking lot for the Greyhound Bus Terminal. There was a twenty-foot gap in the fence that formed the station's eastern boundary. Four minutes. Charlie led Nix out into the middle and shrugged her pack off, dumping it on a small mound in the snow. All they had to do was start the CD player, turn on the loudhailer, and run. It had been waterproofed with a plastic apron and sticky tape. Unfortunately, the apron wasn't transparent so Charlie had to find the right button by touch. As she lifted the loudhailer from the pack, it toppled off the little mound, contents spilling out. Charlie cursed and reached out to grab the bag.

The mound shifted and sat up. A rotting face stared at her, snow falling away in clumps. She threw herself back as Nix started shouting. The infected lurched to its feet. It was a man in coveralls and a Hi-Vis jacket, one of his legs gashed along its length. Charlie went for her pistol, but the holster was empty. The infected sprang forward and she kicked his damaged leg, tripping him back into the snow. She looked around for her weapon but saw another hand pushing up out of the snow. This could not be happening. Hi-Vis lunged at her but Nix fired the Milkor, slamming him back. The infected howled. A second infected rose from the snow.

"Two's too many," said Charlie. "Run!"

She took her own advice, legs pumping for all she was worth, but Nix kept shooting. A baton round hit Hi-Vis square on, snapping his head back, and knocking him down. The second infected, fat in a ripped raincoat, rushed Nix and they toppled in a tumble of limbs. Charlie started to panic and she ran toward them. Raincoat was clawing at Nix's armor, raking his helmet. She launched herself feet first, crashing into the infected, propelling him away. She landed on top of him. He smelled like a sewer and she pushed herself off.

Hi-Vis barreled into her and she was flung back, falling hard. The man grabbed her around the throat and Charlie fought to breathe. She kicked, punched, and headbutted the thing, then Nix grabbed the man from behind. Charlie crashed her forehead into Hi-Vis's face, over and over again. She felt the cheekbone give way and an eye popped out. Nix dragged the body off. Charlie knelt in the snow, gasping for air. Raincoat was getting to his feet, but she had no strength. Her pistol was lying a few feet away. Scooping it up, she shot Raincoat through the bridge of his nose. The bullet exited in an oily spray. He stayed standing for a heartbeat longer, then sank to his knees, head on his chest.

"Is he dead?" asked Nix.

Charlie shot him again. He didn't move.

She sucked in a breath. "Were you bitten?"

"I don't think so."

"Make sure."

"I wasn't bitten."

She stood and checked him over. The fight had taken up time they didn't have. Without music, the others would have no chance. Charlie checked her watch. The Joker said they had less than a minute. Holstering her weapon, she fastened the clip so she wouldn't lose it again. Stupid mistake. She jogged back to the CD player. The equipment was lying in a jumble on the snow but seemed undamaged. Charlie started setting it up exactly as Gath had shown her.

The transmit button was taped down and there was a little feedback whine as she started the CD player. The music would draw every bag of bones in the neighborhood down on them. Nix stood over her. Where was Willie Nelson? She pressed stop then pressed play again. Nothing. Charlie ripped a hole in the plastic. The light was on but it wasn't playing.

"Your piece of shit fucking crap isn't working!"

Nix spread his hands. "It worked before."

"Make it work!"

He leaned over the machine, stopped and started it a few times, then slid the volume up full. 'Seven Spanish Angels' belted out across the car lot, deafeningly loud. Nix whooped and Charlie smiled. She grabbed her pack.

Gath chewed his lip. He wasn't by nature a worrier, but he was glad in the end Charlie had gone with Nix. Anything could be out there, and the longer it took for them to return the more he fretted. Gath stood with Chen and McCord outside the doors to Track 6. The group was ready to go, the chain unlocked, hanging loosely through the handles. They all had pistols, though Chen also brought her APC9K from Aegis. The submachine gun and McCord's Sig had no suppressor so were strictly a matter of last resort. Chen brought her sword too. 'For emergencies', she said. The plan was to start the generators, not get into a fight, so to that extent, all weapons were for emergencies.

"How long?" asked McCord.

"Not long."

"How long's that?"

Old the cop might be, but eating donuts on the Baltimore Express didn't mean you were a veteran. McCord was far too nervous and letting it show. Wearing riot gear didn't make him any calmer. He was pacing up and down, checking and rechecking his ammunition.

"What's with the sword?" McCord asked Chen. "That what Chinamen use?"

"It is Egyptian."

McCord said nothing, probably because he knew as much about Egypt as he did about China.

"Relax, Sarge," said Gath, "they'll be here soon."

"If they ain't, it's your fault."

Gath resisted the urge to strangle him. "GRACE, how are we doing?"

"One minute 38 seconds behind schedule."

McCord shook his head. "Millions of dollars on a talkin' watch."

"Billions," said Gath.

"Figures. Nothin' the federal government loves more than wastin' other people's money."

Gath didn't bother answering, so McCord went on.

"What's the point in goin' to the moon when we've hungry kids at home? You fellas blew millions on a pen that could write in space and the Commies used a pencil."

"Pencils are dangerous. They break, the bits float around in low gravity, and get stuck in equipment. The Fisher Company made a Space Pen and sold it to the government. They sold it to the Soviets too. 128 dollars each."

"128 bucks for a pen? What a crock."

McCord started pacing again. "What do we do if they don't come?"

"We go anyway."

"And if those things are there?"

"We abort."

McCord snorted. "We should abort now."

"Stick to the plan."

"Plan was for them to be here, Colonel."

"We'll go in one minute, whether they're here or not."

The policeman muttered to himself. Time ticked by. Gath checked the corridor for any sign of Charlie and Nix, but it was empty.

"10 seconds, get ready. Sarge, when I tell you, open the doors."

"What if them things is there?"

"Close them."

Chen held a hand up. It took the others a moment before they heard the pounding feet. Charlie and Nix ran around the corner, sprinting down the length of the concourse. They fell into seats in the waiting area. Charlie pulled down her hood, breathing hard.

"What time do you call this, young lady?" asked Gath.

"Music's on."

"Don't mean them things is gone," said McCord.

Nix ripped off his headgear and took a deep breath. "We saw loads of them, coming through the fence."

Gath grinned. "When you're ready, we're going out."

Charlie and Nix sat for a few seconds more, then gave the thumbs-up.

"Draw your weapons," said Gath. "Open her up, Sarge."

McCord yanked out the chain, pulling the double doors wide while the others aimed their pistols. The platform was empty. It stretched 100 yards to the open air where snow drifted down. Daylight streamed in from glass set into the roof. A train stood on a track to one side, advertising covering the wall on the other. Wendy's Mozzarella Sandwiches, Gillette Heated Razors, iPhone 15 Pro. All the little things that used to mean so much to so many. Corridors ran east and west to other platforms. A few infected milled around in the distance at the open end of the platform. From far away he could hear music.

"This way," said McCord. "They're in the middle."

They set off at a slow jog past pillars and seating. Halfway along the platform, they saw three large brown metal rectangles between advertising for Busch Light beer and Arnold Schwarzenegger selling BMWs. They were marked in red and white. *Do Not Touch, Authorized Personnel Only*. The policeman was panting as he walked to the last of the generators. He stumbled back. An old woman, no more than five feet tall, staggered out, snapping at him with broken teeth. Gath shot her in the chest.

"Why is one still here?" asked Charlie.

"She's deaf," said McCord, looking down at the body. "Couldn't hear the music."

"You know her?"

"Her daughter worked here. Can't remember her name. Stella. Her name was Stella."

"Let's get this done," said Gath.

McCord stepped over the woman's body and moved to the generator. It was stamped with the number 3.

"Runnin' diagnostics."

He popped a panel and went to work. It was an old model, but Gath recognized most of what he saw. A key switched modes, with gauges and meters to measure voltage, current, and frequency. The initiator was a big red button. Gath stood with the others and looked to the far end of the platform and waited.

"We need someone back there in case they get in," said McCord, pointing back at the doors.

Gath frowned. That wasn't part of the plan, but he saw the need. Infected might drift back along those corridors to other platforms and get onto the retail concourse. Why didn't he say so before? Chen ran back. The old cop grunted and turned back to the controls. Gath holstered his weapon and started tapping the pistol grip.

He hated waiting. "How long?"

"Not long," said McCord.

The open end of the platform was 50 yards away. The handful of infected there either couldn't see them or didn't care. Why they weren't drawn to the music, he didn't know. Maybe they were deaf too. There was a lot about White's Disease that he didn't understand. Gath flinched as Generator Three rumbled to life, a red light winking on. It sounded like a tractor.

"They're coming," said Charlie.

Her tone was businesslike, untroubled. A handful of infected at the far end of the platform had started in their direction. The sound faded as the generator went into standby mode and the light turned green. It was quiet again, but the infected kept coming. McCord moved to Generator Two and opened the panel. They waited while he worked, watching the infected approach at a slow walk. When they were 20 yards away, Generator Two roared to life, sounding even louder than the first. A larger group of infected appeared and headed toward them.

"This is going to get tricky," said Charlie.

Generator Two cycled down and went on standby. McCord moved to Generator One, the master in the Daisy Chain. They had to get it running and keep it running. The first infected were 10 yards away. More were coming all the time. Charlie shot one in the head, an overweight woman in a business suit, and took down the other three in quick succession. One shot, one kill. More were coming. Gath joined Charlie, shooting slowly and steadily, thinning the herd. He aimed center-mass, taking one or two chest shots to bring the things down. Nix moved beside him and raised the Milkor.

"Get back," said Gath.

"I can hit them."

"Do as you're told!"

Nix bowed his head and moved back.

Gath waved at him. "Stand behind us but keep that thing loaded, OK?"

Nix nodded. There were more than a hundred on the platform now, and the flow was speeding up. They were howling, hissing. No matter how many died, more filled the gaps. They didn't have enough bullets for all of them.

"We have to go!" shouted Charlie.

Gath glanced back at McCord. "A little longer."

"I'm nearly out!"

Gath whistled and passed her a magazine. She reloaded without breaking her streak of headshots. Nix started firing, aiming at the tightly-packed legs. The baton rounds were more effective against slow-moving groups, tripping those that came behind. It wasn't enough. Generator One powered up, the growl of the big diesel machine driving the oncoming mass into a frenzy. Gath couldn't even estimate the numbers anymore, but there were hundreds. They hurled themselves at the defenders, scrambling over the growing pile of dead bodies.

"I'm out!" shouted Charlie.

Gath had no spares, so she stepped back and drew her police baton. Gath could smell them, a mix of blood and shit. He was trying headshots now, and mostly hitting since they were so close. Not many bullets left. His next shot was so close it set a woman's hair on fire. Another blew off a railway worker's jaw, spraying them all with blood. Generator One powered down and the noise faded to just the snarls of the infected. They needed to hold until it started again. Gath fired his last round through the forehead of a pig-faced man in a Taco Bell uniform and then drew his knife.

The little blade wasn't for fighting, but it was all he had. A bang came from behind and the nearest infected fell. McCord stepped forward, pistol in hand. Gath could have kissed him. For a few seconds, only the old policeman stood against the incoming tide, dropping an attacker with every shot. Then he ran out too. Charlie brought her baton down and Gath stabbed with his knife. They beat back every attack, but it couldn't last.

Generator One chugged to life.

"Run!" shouted McCord.

Gath and Charlie took a step back, then ran. With a roar, the infected surged after them. Nix was ahead, Charlie neck and neck with McCord. Gath was at the back, expecting to be brought down by the infected at any moment. There was a loud burst of gunfire ahead. He felt a round zip past his head. Chen stood at the doors, firing in controlled bursts. She switched targets, shooting along the west corridor. Nix turned to help the old cop who was flagging. They reached the doors.

Gath was last inside, and he turned to look back. A wave of infected surged toward him. Chen fired a burst as Nix and Charlie slammed the doors. McCord slid the chain through and closed the padlock. Dozens of bodies hit the other side, shaking the doors. The five of them stood there, breathing hard. McCord collapsed into a seat and Gath slid to the floor.

Chapter 13

H Street was a Hallmark Christmas card, smothered in snow under a pale sky. Pretty, but colder than sin. Gath pulled his scarf down and spat, the gobbet disappearing in the wind. His stomach rebelled. He had managed to finish some pasta with Teriyaki sauce before they left but it wasn't doing his stomach much good. He was getting old. A hot shower had given him a spring in his step, but it was blotted out by mile after mile of snow. The weather had worsened and they were down to a crawl. Everything ached. They were wrapped up in whatever they could find, mostly H&M pants and sweaters. Gath had his police windbreaker over the top; Charlie and Chen wore heavy maintenance coats.

They needed cold-weather gear and that's what they were looking for. Nix was guiding them to a store that catered to skiers. He struggled ahead in his riot gear. Gath's feet were ice cold in his New Balance runners and he fantasized about finding warm boots. They passed a FedEx van in the middle of the street, the driver's head hanging from a hole in the windshield. Nix hit it square on with a snowball but nobody was impressed. They just wanted the journey to be over. Gath dipped his head in commiseration as he passed the dead delivery man.

"I'm dreaming of hiking boots."

He lifted a leg and shook off the slush. Chen's footwear was equally wet, but she didn't complain.

"Do you know what autoamputation is?" asked Gath.

"Yes."

"It's when you don't have blood flow to your fingers or toes and they fall off."

"Yes."

Chen started walking again as Gath wiggled his toes. He'd pay a million bucks for a warm towel. No point losing a foot while he was looking for better shoes. Gath had stopped outside a restaurant. It took him a while to make out the name under the ice. *DBGB Kitchen.* The outside was blackened and burned. Gath took out his water bottle and drank, checking GRACE's map. Not far. He passed a looted clothing store and a row of cars. The world seemed alien. In his mind, this wasn't Washington, it was somewhere else, another planet. He needed a drink. Chen tugged on his sleeve and pointed back the way they had come. Visibility wasn't great, but he tried to see through the squall.

"What am I looking at?"

"I saw something."

"What?"

"I don't know."

He squinted. "I can't see anything, Chen."

"There is something there."

She was insistent, but all he could see was the same frozen churn. "Infected maybe, or snow."

"Not snow."

"What's wrong?" Charlie called back.

"Nothing!" said Gath.

They moved on. H Street was unrecognizable, but Nix seemed to know where he was going. A few minutes later they passed wrought iron lanterns hanging outside the Grand Hyatt. A row of glass doors was set back from the road under a wide arch, Graffiti sprayed across the brickwork in red. *WE DID THIS.* Giant pots were dotted here and there, the plants gone. Gath saw a body curled near one of the doors, a man bundled in a coat. It was expensive. He had been somebody. Once.

"That's it!"

Nix was pointing at a building on the corner that had seen better days. They crossed the street and gathered around its broken doors. The windows on the first floor were smashed and snow had come to rest through the open doorway. The sign said *Arc'teryx* and featured some sort of dinosaur skeleton, *Transcend the Trail* ran above the broken glass.

"Stuff we need's upstairs," said Nix.

They were at a junction and Gath noticed something orange lying on the far side of the street running north and south. It was outside a bar.

"Wait for me here. Don't go in yet," he said.

"Where are you going?" asked Charlie.

Gath didn't answer and started walking toward the orange object. It was easier to walk because the snow was trampled flat by hundreds of feet. Drawing his weapon, he turned slowly in a circle. Nothing else in sight. Crossing to the bar, he saw the orange object was the shredded remains of a hiking jacket, the kind first responders wore. Broken equipment was strewn about the bloody bones of a body. The attack was recent. He walked back to the others.

"So?" asked Charlie.

"Somebody died."

"A lot of people died."

"Recently. Lots of footprints. Keep the noise down and your eyes peeled."

The doors had fallen so he walked straight into the store. It was a mess, looted and rubbed raw by the elements. Snow piled near the doorway and every broken window.

"Not much left."

"Upstairs," said Nix. "This way."

The young man kicked his way through the garbage and jogged along an aisle of smashed shelving and tattered clothes.

"Slow down," said Charlie.

Nix got to a set of stairs at the rear and turned back to the others.

"There's no one here."

A body fell from the stairwell, dropping straight onto him. They crashed down the stairs. Everyone started yelling. The attacker, a man in a black and red hunting jacket, hissed and clawed at the boy as they rolled around on the floor.

Charlie couldn't get a clear shot. Before Gath could think, Chen stabbed her sword through the infected's back. The tip came out of his chest, clean like it had cut only air. Sagging, the man slid to one side and stopped moving.

"I told you to slow the fuck down," said Charlie.

Nix backed away from the body and stood up.

"It's bite-proof," he said, tapping the riot gear.

Charlie reached between the gaps in his armor plates and gave him a sharp pinch.

"Don't be dumb."

She took the lead and went slowly upstairs, pistol scanning ahead. It was darker, so she clicked on the light. The second floor was much more orderly and still had lots of stuff on the shelves. A limited amount of sun came from the tinted windows, leaving the place in shadow. Gath ran his light along the aisles and displays.

"Jackpot."

The place had everything.

"See?" said Nix.

He pulled off his headgear and ran a hand through sweaty hair.

"I told you so. Didn't I tell you so?"

"Sweep the place in pairs," said Gath. "Once we know we're alone, we can start shopping. Chen, you're with me."

Charlie led Nix down an aisle of waterproof jackets and Gath went in the opposite direction. He walked through a mountaineering display and found a section lined with heavy-duty backpacks. Nix appeared.

"We found someone. Alive, I mean."

Nix showed him to the other end of the retail area. Charlie was standing beside an unremarkable door marked *Staff*.

"She won't open it," said Charlie. "She's holding it closed."

"How do you know it's a woman?"

"She's crying."

Gath knocked on the door.

"Hello?"

There was no reply.

"Are you injured, Ma'am? If you're injured, we can help."

"Maybe we should just leave," said Nix. "Maybe we're scaring her."

"We can't leave. She might be hurt or infected."

"Infected don't cry."

"She might be bitten."

"We've got a safe place with power," said Charlie. "We can't leave her behind."

Gath rapped on the door again. "Ma'am, we're going to come in. To make sure you're safe. We have medical supplies, food, and water. Please stand back."

He could hear her now, whimpering. Gath waved the others back and then shoulder-charged the door. It was cheap and flimsy, breaking in the middle. The woman yelped and scrambled away. Pushing the pieces of wood into the room, Gath shone in his light. The woman was standing at the back, crying and gasping for breath. She was tall, dressed in red ski gear. Gath kept his light on her while Charlie moved closer.

"You're safe, Ma'am. You're safe."

The woman raised a knife and Charlie took a step back.

"We're not going to hurt you," said Gath. "Put the knife down."

The woman stared at her for a moment, then dropped the blade, sinking to the floor. Charlie and Chen hurried in to help and Gath pulled Nix out.

"Let's leave them to it. We can start packing the gear."

They found large gray Bora backpacks which fastened around the waist and over the shoulders. Gore-Tex hiking jackets, inner and outer gloves, heavy-duty waterproof pants, fleeces, ski masks, and reflective goggles. As they sorted through the clothing, Nix looked back toward the office where they found the woman.

"What do you think her deal is?"

Gath shrugged. "Just a survivor. She looked clean, healthy, probably hiding out."

"You think there are more people out there?"

"I hope so, Nix." He smiled. "If the human race's just us, we're in trouble."

They chose different colored gear for easy identification. Gath's was gray and Nix's white. They chose blue for Charlie, red for Chen, and kept black for McCord. Then came the hiking boots and socks. Gath peeled off his own sopping-wet ones, drying his feet, and put on the thick new socks.

"Oh yeah. My feet just had an orgasm."

Nix giggled.

"New boots are going to hurt," said Gath, "wear two pairs of socks on each foot. We'll need plenty of padding."

"What'll I do with the riot gear?"

"Leave it. Too heavy to carry."

When they were almost finished changing, Charlie and Chen appeared with the woman. Blond hair spilled out of her coat over one shoulder, and she stared at Gath with wide eyes.

"This is Gloria," said Charlie.

Gath took off his scarf and smiled. "I'm David. Nice to meet you, Gloria."

The woman didn't say anything. Charlie spoke to her quietly while Chen started changing into her new gear. She gave a rare smile at the choice of red.

"Why do Chinese people like red?" asked Nix.

Chen smiled again. "Good fortune."

"Is that why Chinese money is red?"

"Only the 100 note is red. We have many lucky things in China. Number eight is lucky too."

Nix put on his new goggles. "So giving someone 88 Chinese dollars is lucky?"

"100 is luckier."

"Because it's red?"

"Because it's more."

Charlie was helping Gloria pick out gear for herself while she got changed. When everyone was suited up, the woman was Chen's twin but six inches taller. Gloria kept her own military-style backpack.

"Nix knows a few likely places nearby that might have food. We'll take what we can so we can eat something decent tonight."

"First is a Thai place," said Nix.

Charlie clapped. "I love Thai food."

Nix led them downstairs and out into the snow. Gloria seemed hesitant but Charlie calmed her, talking softly as they went. Gath loved his new gear, especially his boots. Walking was a pleasure again.   Haad Thai was a little farther down the street on the other side. Gath made sure they didn't cross until they were well past the remains of the man he had found. Gloria stared across the street at the orange coat, then looked away. The restaurant was a modest place but hadn't been looted or burned. Gath tried the door, and it swung open. Inside was dusty, but nothing seemed out of place. It was decorated in eye-watering tangerine with stylized trees and hills on the wall in black.

"Me and Chen will check the storeroom. Everyone else, keep your eyes open."

Gath used his weapon light as they moved towards the back of the restaurant. The tables were a bit down market for the center of DC and the chairs a bit too kitsch. Chen drew her sword.

"Watch where you're sticking that thing."

The first back room was for the staff, but the second was locked. A few kicks took the handle off and the mechanism plopped onto the floor. His boots kicked ass. The room was lined with treasure. Canned and dry goods, cooking chocolate, spices, preserved fruit, foil-wrapped instant vegetables. He didn't think much of the place's menu but it was enough to feed them all for days. Some of the contents would take a bit of getting used to, like bamboo shoots and straw mushrooms, but it was amazing how hunger broadened the palate. They couldn't take it all, but they could fill up with enough to allow them to go straight back to Union Station.

When they divided it out, their packs were a little heavier than he was comfortable with, but Gath knew they would need the food. Despite his dodgy insides, his mouth watered at the thought of a Thai Green Curry Chicken. Nix led them back even though Gath knew the way. It made the boy feel useful and he had done a great job getting them here. They retraced their steps to Arc'teryx and walked on passed the Hyatt. Gath felt the tension start to leech away from him. They had cold-weather gear and packs full of food. Mission accomplished.

Nix came to a halt and Charlie turned to see what was wrong. Gath knew. About 20 yards away was a man in the middle of the road. He was big, dressed like a soldier in a tactical vest, combat webbing, and a Yankees cap. An Arabic scarf was wrapped around his face below black goggles. Gath couldn't see a weapon.

"Friend of yours?" asked Charlie.

He shook his head. "Wait here."

Gath moved half the distance and stopped, waiting for the soldier to reciprocate. The newcomer did, walking forward with a swagger and stopping a few feet away. The man's name tape said *Walker*, but he had no insignia or rank. Probably special forces. Gath stood there, waiting for the soldier to say something, but nothing happened.

"David Gath," he said, "US Airforce."

The soldier said nothing for a moment, then took a step closer, coming within a few inches.

"Hello, David." Said an electronic voice. *"I've been looking for you."*

Chapter 14

"It's a machine," said McCord.

Gath sipped his coffee while the old man glared.

"Ain't right."

The robot was motionless, unconcerned that he was the subject of speculation. His baseball cap, goggles, and scarf had been removed, exposing a mechanical head. The face was humanoid, like a crash test dummy in high-grade plastic and steel.

"His name's Walker," said Gath.

"It's a thing, how can it have a name?"

"Ozzy's a thing."

The dog had done a lot of barking when Walker first appeared, but he was tired and taking a rest.

"Ozzy's flesh and blood." The old cop scratched the stubble on his head. "Robots. Ain't right."

Gath had explained to the others what Walker was during the hike back through the city. Nix was in awe and kept staring. Gloria didn't seem to register the robot and was now safely asleep in a spare bunk.

"Explain it to me again," said McCord.

"*Perhaps it would be easier if I explained,*" said an amplified voice from the robot.

Everyone stared at the machine. McCord was horrified.

"This is the scientist, Dr. Wolf," said Gath. "Walker can't talk. Go ahead, Wolf."

"*My name is Dr. Aaron Wolf, Sergeant. I'm speaking through an audio-visual system built into the robot. I don't have much power left, so you'll forgive me for being brief.*"

McCord had gone pale.

"*I had to stay at Aegis when David and his team left. I sent Walker to find them. He is part of our research into biological motion. Trying to build robots that walk like humans.*"

"Humans can walk already," said McCord.

"*We try to create robots with our own characteristics so they can replace us in dangerous situations, like disasters, or war.*"

"Man's made in God's image, he can't be replaced."

"*Walker was the only way I had to find you.*"

"Why didn't you come yourself if it was so important?"

"*Leaving the lab complex at this time would present a Challenge. Walker is the ideal messenger. Tireless, immune to the cold, and he doesn't attract the infected.*"

"Can he kill them things?"

"*Walker can't kill, but he can help in other ways.*"

"Why's he dressed like a soldier if he can't kill?"

"*I work for the Department of Defense so most scenarios we simulate are military.*"

Charlie walked up to the robot and reached out to touch his face.

"How did you find us, Wolf?"

"*Hello, Charlie. The Aegis AI recorded your departure. I created search parameters and Walker did the rest. He has spent the last few days searching a grid pattern of likely hiding places.*"

"Did you find your husband?"

"*No. There was no one left.*"

McCord rolled his eyes.

"*My power supply is almost gone. David, you asked me about Jennifer Lang. I know where she is, or at least where she was. I have been going through the data logs. Dr. Lang left Aegis on a special operation the morning of the attack.*"

"What special operation?"

"*Operation Headhunter. I don't have all the details, but Lang was one of six personnel assigned to data retrieval. Three scientists and their escort. They left for Georgetown University in an M-ATV at 0600. They didn't return. Walker can network with your AI so I'm uploading the information I have. All Aegis personnel have Friend or Foe identifiers to show our locations, but they are short-range. The vehicles are much more powerful. The M-ATV's transponder shows it's still at Georgetown.*"

"What's he talkin' about?" asked McCord.

"I have to find someone," said Gath. "A scientist."

"More scientists."

"*David, I won't be able to maintain this link, but Walker will be an asset. His batteries should last for days. When I get the power back here, I'll re-establish contact.*"

"Is everything OK there, Wolf?"

"*I'll be fine. Use Walker wisely and be safe. Farewell.*"

There was a burst of static then nothing. McCord slowly shook his head.

"So that's it? You're just gonna leave?"

"Not tonight."

"Figures."

Charlie clapped her hands together. "We'll worry about tomorrow tomorrow. We brought back enough food to cook up a storm. Let's get it on."

"I've got a bottle with my name on it," said Gath.

McCord nodded. "Sounds about right. So long as my name's on that bottle too, Colonel."

Gath was sitting at the closest thing he could find to a bar, listening to the closest thing he could find to music. The Johnny Rockets restaurant was on the lowest level of the station. Red, white, and chrome, the décor tried to say 50s retro but instead just said bullshit. Gath sat on a shiny stool, surrounded by brightly colored straws and napkins. A stainless steel mini jukebox was in front of him and he thumbed his way through the selection. Gath sipped whisky from an old-fashioned Coke glass as he listened to Mel Carter. It was awful, so pressed *Rescue Me*.

"Easy listening for the out-of-work astronaut."

He heard footsteps but didn't bother turning around. Claws scraped on the tiled floor and McCord sat in the next chair. He had two steaming bowls that smelled wonderful. Ozzy camped out beside him, looking hopeful for scraps.

"You eatin', Colonel?"

"Drinking."

The policeman set the bowls down. "Eatin's better."

Flat noodles, vegetables, and meat. The aroma wafted up and Gath's mouth watered.

"What's the meat?"

McCord shrugged. "Mystery meat."

"What did it say on the can?"

"Somethin' foreign."

McCord lifted the bottle of Glenfiddich, pulled the stopper, and drank from the bottle. The old man sighed in appreciation and put the cork back in. Gath lifted the fork and tried the noodles. He savored the taste, then shoveled more into his mouth.

"For a cop, you're a hell of a good cook."

"Kid made it. If I cooked, you'd be back on the sauce."

"I'll be back on the sauce anyway. I'm a drunk."

"I'll drink to that."

The old cop grabbed the whisky and took another slug.

"Rude to drink from another man's bottle," said Gath.

"A real drunk would drink whisky from a witch's teat."

"I'll take your word for it."

"'You can change your self-destructive decisions by recognizin' that you alone cannot recover. With help from your higher power, you can'."

Gath knew the quote, from The 12 Steps. "How does drink accord with your beliefs?"

The old man considered the question. "Figure the Lord's a whisky drinker. That's why he made it so good."

McCord started eating.

"What kind of noodles are these?" asked Gath.

"Foreign."

"Kid can cook. Aren't you glad you saved him?"

"Always glad I saved him. Just miss old George." He reached for the whisky and took a swig.

"I don't miss anyone."

"Why not?"

"Don't care much for people. Except for my wife. Ex-wife."

"If you miss her, why's she ex?"

"I wanted her to be happy more than I wanted her to be mine."

McCord said nothing to that and they both ate until the song ended. The old man pressed *Pretty Woman*.

"That's not 50s," said Gath.

"You ain't been payin' attention, Colonel. Most of these songs is 60s."

"It's supposed to be a 50s restaurant."

"Don't believe everythin' you read."

McCord leaned down to feed a ribbon of noodles to Ozzy who made them disappear with a flick of his tongue.

"Why did you come down here, Bill?" asked Gath.

"'Before a higher power can begin to operate you first must believe that it can'."

"So, we're both drunks. What else?"

The older man sighed. "You're headin' out tomorrow."

"That's the plan."

"To find the lady scientist."

Gath nodded.

"You know she's probably dead."

"Probably."

"You could stay here. I mean, we got power."

"I made a promise, have to keep it."

"Figured as much."

They ate together in silence.

"I want you to do somethin' for me," said McCord. "When you go, the kid's gonna want to go with you. Tell him no."

"Why?"

"It's a good bet you won't be comin' back. Kid deserves better. Got a good heart."

The old man eyed his bowl.

"I know one end of a gun from the other. I could go with you."

Gath picked up his glass and drank.

"Gloria's been through a lot. I'll need Nix to stay and take care of her, not a grouchy old train cop. No offense."

"None taken."

"And I'd like you to stay here and guard them. You know this place better than anyone. There's a chance Lexington will find this place. As you say, you know one end of a gun from the other."

McCord looked at Gath, then back to his bowl. He nodded.

"Figures."

Nix was lying in the middle of an open-plan walkway on the mezzanine level. It was a piece of installation art, giant pieces of blown glass sweeping out in a spray of color. The glass was suggestive of different creatures. A shark's fin here, an octopus tentacle there. Gath knew nothing about art and cared even less, but he appreciated the skill of whoever had shaped the glass. That was real craftsmanship. Nix popped his head up and waved as Gath cleared the top of the stairs.

"It's called the Rainbow Sea."

"Yours?"

"I wish. I bet no one ever got to see it this way, lying on the floor of a mall at Union Station. It's like being rich. We can do anything."

They said nothing for a while as Gath admired the glasswork and Nix laid back on the floor.

"Did I tell you why I left Dupont Underground?" asked Nix.

Gath shook his head.

"We hated each other. Thought we were friends. Being friends is easy when you've nothing to lose. Everything was a fight over nothing. There was a screaming match one night, real vicious shit. A girl called Leslie cried for days. Wound up dead, just like that, in her sleeping bag."

Nix paused and Gath waited. He didn't know why the boy was telling him this, but as he was half drunk he was happy to listen.

"We were down to eating moldy Saltines so some of us went out to find food. It was so fucking scary, there were bodies everywhere. People were screaming, we didn't know who was infected and who was trying to get away. Gord and Bizzy were killed in a Lobby Mart. Me and Leon took the bags and ran. When we got back, nobody cared about Gord and Bizzy, they just fought over the food. Next day, me and Leon left."

Gath ran his fingers along a glass mermaid and made no comment. Nix sat up.

"My real name is Arthur. Nix is just made up. I always wanted to be different, but now I'd give anything to be normal. You going to Georgetown in the morning?"

"That's the plan."

"Are you coming back?"

"That's the plan, too."

Nix thought for a moment. "You don't want me to go, do you?"

"I need you here."

"There's no need to make stuff up. It's twice as far as last time, I know I'd make it harder for you. Don't even have the armor anymore."

"I need you to take care of Gloria. She'll need a lot of understanding and Bill's not great at that."

Nix grinned. "No, he's not, is he?"

He lay back down. "I got an offer from Georgetown. Art History. Turned it down so I could be myself. Can I come to say goodbye?"

"Charlie wouldn't forgive you if you didn't."

The team assembled in the Great Hall in the morning. Gath had a headache but was otherwise none the worse for wear. Chen and Charlie were up early, already preparing their gear. He hadn't asked them to come, they hadn't even discussed it. He wanted to give them both a big hug but settled for making a dirty joke. Charlie laughed and Chen didn't understand, which made it funnier. They packed eight Thai energy bars that had the usual ingredients plus, for some reason, rice. It wasn't Gath's first choice of snack, but it would keep them alive.

After the fight for the generators, they were low on ammunition. There was enough for one short firefight. They would have to avoid the infected and not use bullets they would need if Lexington found them. Nix was standing with McCord, Ozzy, and Gloria. He was paler than usual, on the verge of tears. The young man knelt to pet Ozzy who rolled onto his back for a tummy rub. Gloria walked towards Gath and gave a hesitant smile.

"How are you feeling," asked Gath.

"Better. I wanted to thank you for saving me."

"We've all been saved by someone."

She held out a small silver key. "This is the key to our RV. 1726 Wisconsin Avenue, behind the pawn shop."

"Thanks, but we'll be walking."

Gloria smiled again. "I know you'll be walking, but the RV has everything. Power, supplies, the lot. If you get cut off and you've nowhere else to go, get to the RV. Her name's Dorothy."

Gath was going to refuse because one extra thing to think about was one too many, but he reached out and took the key anyway.

"Thanks, Gloria."

With the sound of zippers sliding home, the team was ready. The human members, anyway. Walker strode into the room and came to a stop. It was eerie to see something mechanical do such a perfect job of emulating a human. His body language, however, was only fluent when he was walking. The rest of the time his movements were jerky and spasmodic. Gath had replaced Walker's headgear and he looked like a soldier again. The robot would lead them to the M-ATV's transponder. Immune to the freezing temperatures and able to carry 500 lbs. on his back, Walker was their workhorse as well as their guide. Gath held up a hand in greeting.

"Ready to go?"

The machine didn't respond, which wasn't surprising as he couldn't speak. This was going to take some getting used to. Chen and Charlie moved towards the inner doors. Nix and Gloria hurried forward and hugged them both. McCord held back, his face grim.

"It'll take most of the day getting to Georgetown," said Gath. We'll find somewhere to spend the night, then be back tomorrow. If we're lucky, we won't be alone."

Charlie opened the inner doors and Ozzy barked.

"Walker, you go first, you're our guide," said Gath.

The machine just stood there. Gath pointed to the door.

"Go."

The robot seemed to process for a moment, then strode forward. Charlie opened the outer doors and a cold wind blew into the station. Walker marched past her and the others followed, out into the great white nothing.

Chapter 15

The storm struck almost immediately. Clouds roiled overhead and the wind hit them like a hammer. Tons of snow churned into the air. By the time they passed the Smithsonian, they could hardly see and navigation was impossible. For humans, anyway. Walker seemed to have no difficulty finding his way using more arcane means. Gath blessed their new cold-weather gear. There was no way they would have made it through this in hand-me-down coats and scarves from the gift shop. Gath lost sight of the robot up ahead and a sense of loneliness settled upon him.

He twisted to catch a glimpse of Charlie's blue parka, but she was lost in the maelstrom. Getting to Georgetown through a blizzard would take all morning. The first leg would follow the same route they had taken the day before, but after Arc'teryx, they were in uncharted territory. It wouldn't be far to the White House and the center of the battle for DC. A battle they lost. How had they been beaten? He still couldn't believe it. The transponder they were tracking showed Lang's M-ATV hadn't moved, but it didn't tell them why. She might be in danger, she might be dead. Might be anything.

Gath wiped GRACE's screen to see where they were. Outside the National Guard Memorial Museum. He peered through the swirl of snow to try and find his bearings, but it was useless. A box truck appeared out of nowhere. *Shred-it* was printed on the side in big blue letters. *Making sure it's secure.* The wind died down as they trudged on, allowing Gath glimpses of cars, buildings, and something ahead on the road. It was big, lying across two lanes, covered in snow. Like a huge sleeping creature. Charlie and Chen caught up with him.

"What the hell is that?" asked Charlie.

"Whatever it is, it wasn't there yesterday."

The thing on the road was familiar, but he couldn't fit the pieces together. Gath moved toward it. This part of the road was open as it flowed into H Street, the shadows of office blocks pressing in on them. Part of a nearby building had collapsed, the roof sagging at one end. All of a sudden, he knew what it was.

"It's a helicopter."

Charlie looked at him like he was crazy.

"It's on its side. Hit the building and went down. Snow fell on it from the roof."

The scene was clear to him now. Its tail section sheared off. In one piece it was probably 60 feet long, a navy Seahawk or a Super Puma. Chen shouted something that Gath didn't hear. She recognized it too. The Chinese pilot moved closer and shouted.

"Military."

Gath nodded.

They started clearing snow from the downed machine. When there was enough of the body visible to climb up, Gath found some handholds and hauled himself onto the fuselage. Wind buffeted him and he crouched low to stay steady. The rotor blades and mast had been torn away. This lady had seen better days. He moved on all fours to the engine cowling and wiped it with a gloved hand. It was painted with a large US flag. Gath cleared off more snow. The top section of the helicopter was white, the rest olive drab. Chen appeared and examined the exposed paintwork. Neither could see the other's face under the ski masks, but they were both pilots and were thinking the same thing. Charlie climbed up.

Gath crawled to the wheel faring. It covered half the length of the body. He ran a hand across to expose white lettering. *United States of America*. He said nothing and moved to the front of the aircraft. He felt around for the emergency exterior door release, twisted, and pulled. It opened on smooth hydraulics in two sections, the bottom complete with stairs and handrails. As the helicopter was on its side, the stairs were of no use. Gath drew his pistol and clicked on the light, aiming it down. There wasn't much to see inside, an access area with a blue curtain and a scatter of objects on the floor. Holstering his weapon, he dropped down, the bulkhead shifting a little but holding firm.

The entranceway smelled of aviation fuel. He drew his pistol. Everything was at a 90-degree angle. The cockpit door was closed. His light ran along the length of the curtain, hanging down like washing on a line. Gath slid a hand under the curtain and slowly lifted it. He had never been inside a Sikorsky VH-92, a White Top. They were quite new, the latest in secure executive transports flying out of Joint Base Anacostia-Bolling. The passenger cabin was bigger than he expected, with two long couches on one side and two individual seats for VIP passengers on the other. There was a small unlit lamp, fixed in place, and a window framed by miniature blue curtains.

Everything was on its side, so what had been the deck of the aircraft was now the left wall. He made his way along the backrests of the couches which now served as a floor and ducked under the VIP seats jutting out at head height. His light fell on bodies sprawled on the couches covered in papers and items knocked loose by the crash. Men in business suits. They lay face up, spattered with gore. Gath checked inside the jackets and found empty shoulder holsters. A woman in a gray pantsuit was strapped into one of the VIP seats, head lolling, arms hanging down. There was a large wound to her neck that didn't bleed. The other VIP seat was empty.

Gath moved back to the entranceway and then to the cockpit. The door was unlocked but only opened halfway before hitting something. Pushing had no effect, so he squeezed his head and weapon through. The cockpit was badly damaged, the reinforced glass smashed, and the frame bent inwards. The pilot was still strapped into his seat, a long piece of metal pinning him in place through his helmet. The other seat was empty. Gath took a closer look at the dead man. His unit patch said *HMX-1* and *1ˢᵗ* with a cross of yellow rotor blades. The name tape read *PJ Jennings, Col, US Marines*. His sidearm was gone. Gath stepped back and closed the door, letting Colonel Jennings rest in peace.

Charlie dropped down and then helped Chen.

"Three in the cabin, one in the cockpit. All dead," said Gath.

"There must be a base out there," said Charlie. "How many bases in DC?"

"Ten."

"What's the nearest?"

"McNair, but it doesn't matter. You only fly in this weather if you've got no choice. Wherever they came from isn't there anymore."

Charlie stared at him and then nodded. She and Chen moved into the cabin, checking the bodies and talking in low tones.

"Bandage rolls, an inhaler, some bobby pins," said Charlie. "Stick deodorant. Schmidt's, Lavender and Sage."

Gath made his way toward them as Charlie put the finds into her pocket.

"Looks like one of them was infected and attacked the others."

Gath reached up to the dead woman in the VIP seat, lifting her chin. It wouldn't move, rigor mortis locking the muscles in place. She was black, in her 30s or 40s, with tightly braided hair pinned back in a style he didn't know the name of. He searched her clothes, smearing his gloves with blood. Two 100 Dollar bills, a name card, tissues, and a box of mint Tic Tacs. Gath read the name card aloud.

"Erin Wilson, Deputy Chief of Staff to the Vice President." He looked up at Charlie and Chen. "It's Marine Two."

Marine Two was the helicopter used by the Vice President. Gath pointed to the empty seat opposite the dead woman. There was a circular seal embroidered into the headrest cover. *Vice President of the United States*.

"Maybe she wasn't onboard," said Charlie.

"She was onboard. The weapons are gone, so there were at least four survivors."

"Why four?"

"They took the weapons. The co-pilot had his own, so three more were unarmed. At least four survivors."

Gath ducked beneath the body in the seat and negotiated his way to the rear. Military designs were built to type, so it wasn't hard to find the emergency locker. Empty except for a box of red parachute flares. He tucked a couple into a pouch on his pack.

"Emergency gear's gone."

"We need to find them before they freeze."

"No. Lang's the mission."

"We can't just leave them out there, David."

"The vaccine's all that matters."

"But it's the Vice President."

Gath didn't reply. He moved out to the entranceway and climbed up out of the hatch. A gale was blowing, buffeting him as he reached down for the others. When they re-emerged, Gath led them across the belly of the helicopter as the wind shrieked overhead. They dropped off the side. Walker was standing a few yards away like he was expecting them. Gath pointed towards Georgetown, and the robot strode off into the swirling snow, Charlie and Chen in his wake. Gath was left alone. He looked at the wreckage for a long moment, then followed his companions.

Visibility deteriorated and it was difficult to see more than a few steps ahead. They took a branching road onto H Street, bunching up to keep each other in sight. If anyone fell out of line, they would get separated and be impossible to find. A steady barrage of sleet made every step forward a battle. Walker was unconcerned and marched like he was in a parade. Gath's had trouble focusing. He wiped the goggles and sighed. Wandering wastelands was a young man's game. At 48, it was a toss-up which body part was going to fail first.

They reached Arc'teryx and then headed into the unknown. Anything could be waiting for them at the center of the city. An armed Aegis expedition had already failed to return. They passed the red columns and pagoda rooves of Chinatown, but Chen didn't give it more than a glance. Gath's legs were starting to ache. Pushing his old limbs two days in a row was beginning to tell. He rubbed one thigh and felt better until he realized he had lost sight of Chen. Had he been left behind? Panic welled up in him for a moment, then he forced it back down. He called her name but his words were snatched away by the wind. A figure in red materialized from nowhere.

"What is it?" asked Chen.

Gath's relief was immense. "I'm just old."

Charlie appeared. "What's happening?"

"He is old," said Chen.

Gath tried to recover his dignity by moving into the lead. He couldn't see the robot, but the tracks were clear enough. The buildings were taller now. Washington DC was famous for restricting the height of buildings, but this close to the heart of government they were usually ten or twelve stories. He passed a stylized flame on a black awning. *Fire & Sage*. Gath didn't know what it sold, but the picture made him feel a bit warmer. He realized he knew the area. The American Association for the Advancement of Science had invited him to a conference in this neighborhood. It stuck in his mind because the liaison had been astonishingly beautiful. Gath had spent most of the extremely boring conference looking at her.

It was easy to feel small as they passed the portico of a church at the junction of H Street and New York Avenue. The blizzard had eased enough to see the red stone walls and white tile running off into nothing. Gath couldn't remember its name. He passed a burned-out Potbelly Sandwich Shop and his stomach rumbled. Oh for a Grilled Chicken Club and nuggets. Gath reached into a pocket for one of the Thai energy bars, ripping off the wrapper. It wasn't a taste sensation but wolfed it down. Looking for a trashcan he remembered he didn't need to anymore, and he let released the plastic into the wind.

Walker was ahead. The robot had stopped. As the others caught up, the machine raised an arm and pointed. A line of Abrams Tanks blocked the road.

"GRACE, are you picking anything up?"

The computer's little speakers weren't up to the wind, so GRACE flashed a negative response onto the screen. As they moved closer, they saw there was a long line stretched into the swirl of snow in both directions. Approaching the nearest, he saw a dead body in a turret. The machines were frozen in place. Nothing here but old bones. Gath reached out and rapped the armor. Homogenous steel plates over layers of depleted uranium and ceramic. Grabbing a handrail, he pulled himself up onto the side and then climbed onto the turret, crouching to ward off the wind. The body beside him had been badly mauled and he looked away. Visibility was better up here. He could see more tanks cordoning off Lafayette Square to protect the White House. It hadn't worked. The White House was gone.

"What's wrong?" called Charlie.

He shook his head and climbed down the other side, dropping into the snow. He was in a command post, with tents and support vehicles. There were a few more corpses.

Charlie climbed down beside him and leaned close.

"The White House."

Gath just nodded.

"Check for weapons and ammo."

He checked the command post, coming up with a Gerber knife and a Sig M17 pistol with no bullets. Gath stuffed them in his pack. Chen dropped from another tank.

"Nothing in the tanks I checked. Walker went around."

Gath hadn't seen the robot do any climbing yet so he guessed it wasn't his thing. Charlie nearly lost her footing as she climbed back down.

"Just empty magazines. Why did they get out of the tanks?"

"If you surround it with enough bodies, tanks can't move. The main gun isn't much use up close. Once they ran out of machinegun ammo and rations, it's either run or starve."

Hell of a choice. They reached another roadblock 10 minutes later and climbed over. They found Walker waiting on the other side. Gath gave the robot a little wave.

"Don't like heights? When we're back I'll ask Wolf to give you an upgrade. Change your name to Climber."

The robot tilted his head as the humans laughed and headed off again on the road to Georgetown.

Chapter 16

The storm had passed, the midday air crisp and clear. They were on a downward-sloping road looking across to a football field full of army tents. The empty encampment ran in rows of olive drab hemmed in by snow. It was deserted. Buildings ringed the fences around the giant rectangle, houses, dormitories, ground maintenance, and a pavilion. They weren't up high enough to see between the tents, so they would have to search each little alley to find Lang's transport. A plastic bag skittered into view, caught by the breeze.

"Why would scientists go to a football field?" asked Charlie.

Gath gestured for Walker to go on. "You can ask when we find them."

The robot loped down to an open side gate and stopped. There was more fencing inside, funneling visitors in different directions on game days. A blue and white sign said *West Section, East Section*, with arrows going both ways. Gath peered through the shiny chain link. Tiered seating was at both ends, the tip of uprights sticking up over the tents. A brick wall rose high at the back with *We Are Georgetown* in man-sized letters. Vehicles were clustered nearby, none of them an M-ATV. Some were military, some civilian. The civilian SUVs screamed 'unmarked government vehicle'.

"Dumb to put tents up when you have all these buildings," said Charlie.

"It's the army way. They go by the book and the book says tents."

"No initiative?"

"None. Follow orders, then fuck-ups are owned by someone else."

"You think Lang's still alive?"

"I stopped thinking."

Gath followed the chain link channels towards the western section, passing the main gate. There was a white Ford van, two army 5-ton trucks, and an Oshkosh HEMTT transporter with an empty flatbed. The HEMTT was a heavy hauler used for large-scale combat re-supply or moving other vehicles. Right inside the open metal gate was a hut with *Hoyas, The Gameday Store* painted on it. A sign had been riveted to the wooden wall. *41st Medical Detachment,* with a red cross and an Asclepius. Gath led them passed a red brick structure with double doors to a green fence. A few kicks buckled the gate inwards. It felt good to break something after all this walking, though his thigh still ached.

Gath moved to the nearest tent and ducked inside. There wasn't much in the half-light, empty MREs, water bottles, and a few bedrolls. One was stained red. Gath left and walked farther into the camp. There were outsized tire tracks in the snow and lots of footprints. Giving a hand signal to the others, he drew his pistol. Gath came to a cooking area opposite a laundry. The tracks ran through it, bent pots and pans scattered here and there.

"A lot of infected."

Charlie examined the footprints. "How do you know they're infected?"

"Some are in bare feet."

They moved through a latrine area, the sour smell still clinging to the cold air. There was a body lying across the tire tracks, dressed in white camouflage. Gath signaled the others to wait and crept forward between the gap in the green vinyl walls. The corpse was quite fresh, lying on top of the snow, not partially buried. It was a soldier, in winter camouflage with gray combat webbing. Gath pulled the man's hood back and unbuckled his helmet. Lifting off the face covering and goggles, he found himself looking at a black man in his 30s. His face was battered, the neck livid with bruising.

He ran a gloved hand down the neck. Gath felt pulped vertebrae, moving under the skin like a broken bird. Unzipping the parka, he exposed the uniform beneath. *Military Police* was on the black Kevlar vest with the chevrons of a corporal.

"Mapuya," said Charlie, reading the name tape. "Is he on the list?"

Gath nodded. GRACE had downloaded the list of personnel assigned to Operation Headhunter. Chen lifted a submachine gun from the snow, another APC9K. This one was different, with a chunky suppressor and an accessory on the back of the Picatinny rail. Gath went through the man's pouches, coming up with two submachine gun magazines, a first aid kit, and two ration bars. They were Soldier Fuel energy bars, used in MREs. The magazines were translucent, allowing ammunition levels to be seen at a glance. Gath passed the magazines to Chen.

"How did he die?" asked Charlie.

"Broken neck. Like something heavy fell on him."

"The M-ATV?"

"Unlikely."

"Lexington shoot and the infected bite. Who breaks necks?"

"We need to find the others. Two more MPs and the science team."

"Let's hope broken necks aren't catching."

They moved on, through the demolished tents. Charlie had Chen's SMG, while the Chinese pilot used the one with the suppressor. It didn't take long to find the M-ATV. It had broken through metal fencing and ended up in some kind of hole. Rear wheels were suspended a few feet off the ground, the body of the vehicle sloping downwards. There were two hatches in the back in the assault configuration. Gath signaled for Charlie and Chen to follow him as he moved closer. The M-ATV was non-standard, bigger, the white bodywork smeared with gore.

"Keep away from the blood, even in gloves."

"Big gun," said Charlie.

"A CROWS turret. Operated from inside."

"Wish we had one of those."

"We do now."

The air had a taint to it. Gath bent to look into the two-foot gap between the edge of the pit and the side of the vehicle. A shriveled face stared back at him. It was dead but the white eyes were still open. There were other infected too, lying on rows of body bags and corpses wrapped in dirty linen.

"It's a mass grave."

Charlie peered down. "I didn't think we did mass graves."

Gath unbuckled his pack and slung it over Walker's shoulder. He didn't seem to mind, and his posture didn't change. Gath holstered his pistol and jumped down between the armored hide of the M-ATV and the side of the pit. Footing was uneven and something in the body bag he stood on broke apart. Gripping the handle of the passenger door, he twisted and heaved himself up. The smell was worse inside. There was a fading red emergency light, and someone slumped beside the steering wheel on the driver's side. They wore the same winter camouflage with combat webbing like the other body. This one had no headgear.

It was a woman, face tilted away. Gath leaned closer. Her auburn hair was tied back in a bun, caked with blood on one side. There were two seats in the front, three facing rearward, and six more in two rows along each side at the back. Gath climbed into the rear and checked the lockers for stowed gear. They were almost full. There was an Improved First Aid Kit, a Combat Lifesaver Bag, MREs, ration bars, bottles of water, signal flares, and four magazines for the APC9K. Gath climbed back to the front seat and called out of the open door.

"Pass down my pack."

When he loaded in his finds, the bag was pretty heavy. He passed it out to Charlie.

"Divide it up and put the MREs in Walker's pack."

Gath steeled himself to search the dead woman. Being with the body in the confines of the vehicle was a little too intimate. Her weapon and ammunition were gone, but she had lip balm, gum, hand cream, two Q-tips, and a ration bar. He left them. Unzipping her parka, he checked the name tape. *Erlich.* Judging by the gore around the windshield and the door, she had died in the crash, but he was no expert. He left her in peace and exited the vehicle.

Charlie passed him his pack, which was substantially lighter.

"The body in the front's another soldier," said Gath. "Erlich. Probably died in the crash."

"That leaves one MP and three scientists. We can't track them through this if we don't know where they went," said Charlie.

"You want to go back?"

"If we can't find them, we should go back to the helicopter."

Gath didn't want to leave, but Charlie was right. The transponder was their only lead and now they had nothing. Lang could be anywhere.

"Look," said Chen.

She had the new submachine gun in her hands, examining the screen mounted on the back rail. Gath got up and stood beside her. The screen was on, showing tiny letters and red dots.

Gath squinted. "What am I looking at?"

"The red dots are us. They move when we move. I think the letters are the people we are looking for."

Gath's mood changed on a dime. "Wolf said Aegis personnel had Friend or Foe chips."

Chen nodded. "There is an E near us and an M 120 feet behind."

"Erlich and Mapuya."

"The others are farther away, close together. L and P."

"Lang and there's a Dr. Prashad on the team."

"They are 300 feet to the northwest."

She pointed to a building on a hill overlooking the football field. Gath craned his neck to get a better look. It was an old Gothic-style place.

"Captain Chen," said Gath, putting his pack back on. "Go to the top of the class."

"I don't understand."

"I'm promoting you to General. Come on."

It took another ten minutes to find a passable route through the camp to the north end of the field. Coming to a gate in the chain link fence, Gath paused.

"Chen, call out 'Contact' if you see any red dots on the screen that aren't us."

The gate was locked so he kicked it open and went through another gate, up a flight of decorative stone steps. The building was old and imposing, with six stories of alcoves, buttresses, and arched windows. It had a foreboding feeling to it.

"Which floor are they on?"

Chen checked the device. "It does not vertically differentiate."

"OK, we won't be picky. We'll go to the same spot on each floor until we find them."

"I don't like the look of the place," said Charlie. "It's got gargoyles."

"That's an owl."

"I still don't like it."

"We won't be long."

Gath walked to the glass double doors. They were quite handsome, framed in lacquered wood. The windows were plastered on the inside with posters. Event advertisements and notices to students. *The GU Rollers, 8 tonite, Pavillion - Karaoke Saturday 9th, No Alcohol, Seniors' Lounge - University Mass for the late Katherine Best, Monday December 11, 4:30pm, Dahlgren Chapel.*

"I don't like this," said Charlie.

"We're not going back because you don't like the architecture."

"There's something wrong with the place."

The door was unlocked and opened without a sound. Gath lifted his mask and sniffed the air. Musty, but nothing suspicious. They were in a dimly lit entrance hall, very spacious. The windows were covered by heavy curtains, with a few cracks letting in a little light. The floor was wide with black and white tiles, like a giant checkerboard, stretching into the dimness. A registration desk was in front of the paneled wall on the right, with two old-fashioned elevators beside it and then a grand staircase leading up. Hallways ran off in two directions.

"It's like a horror movie," said Charlie. "I hate horror movies."

They took off their masks and goggles. Gath drew his pistol, activated the tactical light, then walked over to the nearest elevator and pressed the button.

"They aren't on," said Charlie. "The button didn't light up."

Gath pressed it again. He didn't hear the hum of the mechanism.

"We'll take the stairs," he said.

"Those stairs?"

"There aren't any other stairs."

"I'm not going up those creepy-looking stairs. Let's take a hallway. We need to check this level before we go up."

"We have to go west," said Chen.

"Which way's west?"

"Left," she said, pointing.

"Walker, you go first."

As if reluctant, the robot didn't move, then it lurched to life, leading them off into the dark.

Chapter 17

The hallway was pitch black. Their tactical lights tracked in all directions, picking out shabby paintwork and bare bulbs hanging from the ceiling. Walker led the way with a self-assurance that the humans didn't share.

"Can he see in the dark?" asked Charlie.

Gath peered over the robot's shoulder. "I hope so."

The first floor was an admin level, with doors marked *Registrar*, *Student Advice*, and *Equality, Diversity, & Inclusion*. Walker stopped a few feet from the end. There was a covered window and a simple set of white-painted steps going up. Someone had gone to a lot of effort to block out the light, plastering the glass with hundreds of pieces of paper, wadded into a paste. It looked like someone chewed and spat out each piece. Classy. Chen tapped the screen mounted on her weapon rail.

"This is the location."

Gath shone his light at the very last door before the stairs. *Medical Office* was stenciled in gold paint.

"Are you going to open it?" asked Charlie.

He tried the handle, but it was locked. It took three kicks before the door banged open. Dust floated through the beam of his light as he peered in. A desk, a sink, and two narrow beds. It smelled faintly of iodine. To one side there was a privacy screen leaning against the wall and a cabinet with medication, bandages, and ointments. Treatment for bumps, bruises, and diarrhea. Nothing important enough to carry. There was something depressing about the room. It reminded him of the nurse's office when he was a boy. The woman had smoked, and her room always stank.

"Next floor."

There was enough space for two to go up, side by side.

"Don't ask me to go first," said Charlie.

"I won't."

"These stairs should be condemned."

"Old university buildings don't need to be to code. They're landmarks."

"And half of Congress went to the same school."

"Walker, how are you with steps?" asked Gath.

The machine immediately started up the stairs in slow, jerky motions. He smashed walking out of the park, but in everything else, he was a Tonka Toy. Gath waited for the robot to get a decent head start, then followed, one hand on the metal rail. Whatever Walker's eyes were made of, he didn't put a foot wrong in the dark. Gath called out for the robot to stop on the second floor. There was another window covered in the same way. This time the door nearby said *Gender Neutral Showers*.

"Chen, keep an eye out for red dots."

She didn't need to be told, but he was nervous. Gath pushed the door open. There were eight white tiled shower stalls with drawn green plastic curtains. Gath searched the first few. A little old-fashioned but clean. Notices on the walls said *Please Wear Clothes in the Hallway* and *One Person Per Stall.* He left the room and directed Walker to continue to the third floor. Similar layout with more showers, unlocked and empty. Gath caught a whiff of something as he left the stalls, something rancid. He walked along the hallway a little, his light brushing the dormitory doors. The smell didn't get any stronger, so he went back.

"Can you smell that?" he asked.

Charlie sniffed. "Like old garbage. Chen, does that gizmo work on movement?"

"Gizmo?"

"The thing on your gun. It shows movement?"

"Yes."

"What if the infected aren't moving? What if they're waiting?"

"Waiting?"

"For us."

"They don't think," said Gath. "They can't. Anyway, trust your eyes and ears. But if Chen sees a load of red dots, we'll run in the opposite direction."

Walker led them up to the fourth floor and the smell returned, getting steadily worse as they climbed. The shower door was ajar. The stink was awful. Humans evolved to keep away from bad smells, shit, vomit, and death, a basic warning system to avoid disease. Gath could smell every one of them now. He nudged open the door with his boot and ran his tactical light along the stalls. The curtains were closed, grimy, and spattered with old blood. Though every instinct told him to keep out, he stepped inside. The floor was sticky, and he shone his light down. Dried gore caked the tiles.

Gath moved to the nearest stall and eased the curtain aside. A body hung from the shower fixture, suspended by a chain wrapped around the chest and under its arms. The metal pipe had been bent upwards to prevent it from sliding off. It was a woman, though that was a guess based on long hair and a slight build. She had been dead for weeks. Her head hung down to a chest stripped of flesh. The genitals were gone. Gath vomited. What remained of noodles and half a ration bar splashed onto the floor. He heard Charlie throwing up in the hallway. Wiping his mouth, Gath took a drink from his water bottle and spat it out.

It wasn't easy to look again, but he had no choice. Gath examined the wounds on the corpse more closely. Gashes. Chewed, mangled flesh. Teeth marks and large bites. Like a bear attack. But bears didn't eat people or hang them in shower stalls. Sadness overcame him. He was glad he couldn't see her face, then felt ashamed. The woman deserved to be remembered. Gath lifted the chin The face was unmarked and she seemed at peace. He lowered her head. There were three more stalls on this side, four on the other. Moving to the next, he lifted the plastic.

Another woman, long dead. She must once have been really overweight, the flesh of her belly sagging like a skirt.

Large chunks were missing from the skin, shapes cut in cookie dough. The head hung back. Her eyes were closed, the jaw broken and slack. Like she was screaming. It was Chen's turn to vomit. Gath went to the next stall. A younger woman, the body fresher than the others, dead maybe a week or two. She was tall, her legs touching the filthy tiles of the floor.

"Which one is Lang?" asked Charlie, her voice barely a whisper.

"None of them. They've been dead too long."

Without a word, they stared at the other five stalls with the curtains still drawn. Feeling hollow, Gath moved to the last on this side. Empty, with a fragment of used soap. Gath crossed to the first of the four stalls opposite and pulled back the curtain. The corpse there was fresh, dead in the last day or two. She was young, with light brown skin. Some of the hair was gone now, ripped off with a clump of the scalp. More than half her flesh had been gnawed away. Charlie threw up again.

"Is it Lang?" asked Chen.

"GRACE, do you have a photo on file for Dr. Lang?"

"*Yes, David, and the records contain a description.*"

"Go ahead."

"*Jennifer Louise Lang, female, 40 years old, African American, 5'6", 130lbs.*"

Gath looked at the picture. It wasn't the woman in the stall.

"Do you have one of Dr. Prashad?"

He compared the photo to the body.

"It's her. She was 28."

Charlie was suddenly furious and she swept aside the next curtain to find another empty stall. Gath made no move to stop her as she yanked open another. He could see her anger drain away. Inside was a skull and most of a ribcage, skin almost rotted from the bone. There was a dried-out mess around the drain. Charlie was crying now, releasing grief she had pent up for days. Gath drew back the final curtain to finish this. A woman's body hung from the shower pipe. Her arms and legs had been bitten and there was blood and shit caked around the drain. The corpse was less brutalized than the others, dead less than a day. She was black. Her head dangled forward, defying identification, but Gath knew who it was. He lifted her chin as gently as he could and shone his weapon light into her face.

"Is it her?" asked Chen.

"Yes."

Gath kept his hand under her chin, staring at the dead woman, thinking of everyone who had died to get them there.

"Let's go back to the helicopter," said Charlie.

The woman's eyes snapped open, and she screamed. Gath jerked back, dropping his pistol. The light clicked off and everything went black. Chen's weapon light snapped on a second later and the woman looked up.

"Get me down," she whispered.

Gath lifted the woman off the shower pipe, passing her out to Charlie and Chen. Together they carried her into the hallway and lay her on the linoleum floor. Charlie opened a water bottle and poured some into her mouth. The woman spluttered but managed to keep some down, then closed her eyes. Chen opened her pack and took out a survival blanket from the Combat Lifesaver Bag and emptied out a first aid kit. Covering the naked woman with the blanket, she and Charlie started tending to the wounds as best they could. Gath kneeled beside her.

"Are you Jennifer Lang?"

The wounded woman said nothing and didn't move. Charlie unwrapped a fentanyl lollipop.

"Take this. It will make you feel better."

The woman opened her eyes.

"Give me pills. I want to be awake."

Charlie found the Advil while Gath just stared.

"You know me?" she asked.

"I'm looking for Jennifer Lang."

Charlie gave her a handful of Advil, one at a time, and more water as Chen began disinfecting and bandaging her wounds. The woman laid back after she swallowed the pills and closed her eyes. Charlie helped Chen with the dressings.

"I'm Lang," said the woman.

Gath was still astonished, and he didn't know what to say.

"Thank God you're alive, Dr. Lang. John Barnes sent me."

Barnes had been the Commander of the International Space Station. Lang lay there with her eyes closed.

"More?" asked Charlie.

The woman gave a slight nod. Charlie fed her more pills and water.

"We're patching up your arms and legs. Where else are you hurt?"

"Did you kill it?" asked Lang.

"Kill what?"

Lang closed her eyes. "How many soldiers do you have?"

"We're not here with soldiers," said Charlie, "it's just us. Don't worry, you're safe."

Lang started coughing and Charlie gave her more water. The scientist cleared her throat.

"I'm not safe and neither are you."

"We're going to get you out of here."

"You don't get it. It wasn't a man and there aren't enough of you to kill it."

"Who was it?"

Lang reached up and grabbed her arm. "You're not listening to me. It's a thing. A big fucking thing with teeth. Now get me the hell out of here before it comes back."

"Why are you so scared?" asked Charlie.

"I've been hanging up like a side of beef for three days. I was first, but he doesn't like dark meat. She begged. Every time it came, she begged. Damn right I'm scared and you should be too."

Gath checked the hallway with his light. "We've got weapons."

"So had I. What ammo?"

"9mm."

"PIKE rounds?"

"What do you mean?"

"Your submachine gun's from Aegis. Aegis issued us frangible ammunition. PIKE rounds. Good against infected, bad against armor, shit against that thing out there."

Charlie and Chen pulled out their magazines. Charlie's were normal brass. Chen had rounds with blue tips. She swapped it out with standard ammo from her pouch. They were running very low.

"Look in the dorms for clothes, lots of layers," Gath told Charlie.

"We don't have time for that," said Lang.

"You won't last five minutes outside in a blanket. We're going to get you cleaned up too."

"I'm not going back to that place."

"There's an empty shower on the third floor."

Lang nodded slightly. "I had a notebook with my research in it. It's pink. It's more important than clothes."

Charlie nodded and she and Chen left to search the dormitories. Gath watched the woman on the floor lie there with her eyes closed as the minutes ticked by. Lang opened her eyes.

"This is taking too long."

"This thing," said Gath, "what does it look like?"

"Eight feet tall. It had to bend to get through the door. Picked me up like paper."

"Where are the rest of your team?"

"Dead."

Charlie and Chen emerged holding a bundle of clothes. They set them down beside Lang and set a pink notebook on top.

"We found your snow gear," said Charlie, "but it was in pieces."

Lang picked up the notebook and held it to her chest. "The book's all that matters. Can we leave now?"

"Walker will take you to the showers downstairs."

"Walker?"

The machine took a few steps forward into the light and then slid his hands under Lang, lifting her like she weighed nothing at all.

"A robot from Aegis," said Gath.

Lang stared at Walker's covered face and said nothing. Charlie handed Gath's pistol to him. He had forgotten he'd dropped it. The robot moved to the stairs and went down, moving no slower for the burden he carried. On the third floor, Gath waited outside in the hallway while they washed Lang. It was a relief to be away from the butcher's stink above. Despite what Lang had said, a man had done this. Big, crazy, but still a man. Men could be killed. Gath walked onto the landing and aimed his light down the stairwell. It echoed. He hadn't noticed when the others were with him. There was nothing down there, so he went back to the hallway.

Gath clicked on his tactical light and ran it along the floor and walls. A row of doors, cheap flooring, peeling plaster, dust. Nothing else. Gath relaxed a little and felt his stomach rumble. A giant cannibal wasn't charging at him right now, so there was time for a snack. He sat down on the linoleum and rummaged around in his pack. Bringing out his canteen and a ration bar. The wrapper said *Soldier Fuel*

Energy Bar, Elite Performance Nutrition with a photo of special forces jumping out of a helicopter. *Featured in the official US Special Operations Forces Nutrition Guide.* Bullshit. He ripped it open and bit into the chocolate. A hell of a lot better than the rice ones.

A howl came from the bowels of the building, then faded away. Gath dropped the chocolate bar and picked up his pistol. What the hell was that? His weapon light reached about halfway down the hallway. Breathing in, he tried to calm himself. He stood and edged forward until he could see the end of the hallway. Empty. Jogging back to the showers, he turned to scan the darkness again. Had he imagined it? Gath wasn't hungry anymore. All he could think about was the howl and an eight-foot creature with big teeth.

Chapter 18

"Did you hear that?"

Gath's nerves were fraying as Charlie and Chen came out of the showers.

"What?" asked Charlie.

"A howl."

Lang exited feet first. Walker swung her expertly, missing the doorway by an inch. She wore a hoodie and sweatpants under a raincoat, runners on her feet.

Charlie shone her light along the hallway. "What do you mean a howl?"

"A howl, like an animal."

"What kind of animal?"

"I'm not a howl expert."

"We need to go," said Lang. "Where is your vehicle?"

"We walked," said Gath.

"My wounds are infected, we've no time to walk."

"Infected?"

"Not that kind of infected. Sepsis. Blood poisoning. I need to get to Aegis before it kills me. We can use the Matvee I came in."

"Too noisy."

"It's electric, doesn't make much noise."

The howl came again, a rumble from somewhere below. It sounded closer than before.

"What the hell was that?" asked Charlie.

Gath aimed his light down the hallway. "I told you there was a howl."

"We need to go," said Lang. "Now."

"What is that thing?" asked Charlie.

"I don't know."

"You're a scientist."

"Science is pretty big honey."

"Why does it only eat women?" asked Chen. "All the bodies were women."

No one had an answer.

Gath moved to the stairwell. "There's a Medical Office on the first floor."

"I'm not a trust fund kid with the clap. I need Vancomycin and Tobramycin, intravenous antibiotics, exact dosages. We need to go to Aegis."

"We can't."

"Why not?"

"It was attacked. There's no one left."

Lang stared at him. "That's bullshit."

"It's true, I'm sorry."

"There are 700 people at Aegis."

"Not anymore."

Lang didn't speak for a moment. "Then I need a hospital."

"There are no hospitals," said Charlie.

"There are hospitals, just no doctors. Get me to one, I can do the rest."

"Hospitals would be ground zero during an outbreak. They'll be crawling with infected. We can find somewhere else, like a vet."

"I'm not a dog."

"We can argue when we're out of here," said Gath. "We'll go down to the first floor, get to the entrance hall, then back to the Matvee. Once we're behind all that lovely armor, we can argue about what's next."

Chen held her submachine gun out to Lang, pointing at the mounted screen.

"What is this?"

"A Merson. It uses sound to detect movement. Don't bet your life on it, and definitely don't bet mine."

"We'll use it but we won't rely on it," said Gath. "Chen, you go first."

The Chinese pilot led them down the steps, sweeping her weapon slowly from side to side to detect movement. Gath watched Lang cling to Walker as they descended. The scene in the shower room had sickened him. How could she even function after that? She was hard as nails. As a kid, he had heard stories about ogres eating children. They were still in his head somewhere, rattling around. His mouth was dry, so he took a drink from the water bottle and wished it was whisky. Opening a flap and unzipping an inner pocket, he took out his lucky charm. The Thunderbird 2 keychain hadn't done much for him so far, but he gave it a quick rub with his thumb. It couldn't hurt.

Chen reached the bottom of the stairs without incident, and they bunched up before moving along the first-floor hallway. The mustiness was a welcome relief from the stench above. He felt every creak of the linoleum-covered floorboards. Gath didn't remember it being this noisy on the way in. Their lights hit the edge of the checkerboard tiles as the entrance hall came into view.

Another howl, close now. Everyone stopped, even Walker.

"Doesn't sound human," said Charlie.

"I told you, it's not," said Lang. "You don't listen."

"Anything on the Merson?" asked Gath.

Chen shook her head. Gath wiped the sweat from his eyes. He needed to piss. Chen edged into the entrance hall, and passed the bottom of the staircase, shining her weapon around the room. Gath had a terrible certainty that they were being watched. His light darted along the length of the hall and across the ceiling, but there was nothing.

"Make sure you're on full auto. I'll go first."

They only had a few seconds of ammunition on full automatic, but if something big came at them, they would need to put it down fast. If they could. Gath led the way across the tiled floor. The doors were close, they were going to make it.

"Contact!" shouted Chen.

There was a deafening roar. Every inch of Gath wanted to run, but he couldn't leave the others. He turned to see what had found them. It was immense, towering by the staircase, lit by their weapon lights. Hooded and wrapped in heavy cloth, its body was crisscrossed by chains. It could have walked straight out of any number of nightmares. The thing bellowed and charged, moving with incredible speed. Walker was closest, cradling Lang like a baby. A huge arm swept down.

But Walker wasn't there anymore. He went from a standing start to a sprint in the blink of an eye, whisking Lang out of harm's way. The others opened fire. Rounds peppered the monster, hitting chains and cutting into ridges of muscle. It squealed, high-pitched like a pig, and smashed Charlie away. Chen stopped to change mags and it backhanded her across the floor. They weren't going to stop this thing, but Gath started firing anyway. Taking two great strides in his direction, the creature lashed out. There was no pain, just a sense of weightlessness. Gath hit the wall and slid down.

Then the pain started. Blood poured from his mouth and he couldn't see. There was yelling and the bang of Charlie's unsuppressed weapon. Spitting, Gath moaned and fell onto his front. His whole body was on fire. Breathing was hard, so he rolled onto his side and gulped in a mouthful of air. Gath's eyesight was coming back. The fight raging in the center of the hall came into focus. Flashes of gunfire in the dark turned it all into a flickering old movie. The creature roared like King Kong as bullets tore into it.

Charlie and Chen were shooting from opposite sides of the hall, firing at an angle so they didn't kill each other.

Walker ran through the bursts of light, Lang left somewhere in the shadows. The robot weaved in and out, dodging the great fists that tried to bash him to the ground. Try as it might, it couldn't catch the machine. Giving up, the beast ran at Chen. She stood her ground, insanely brave, and kept firing. The monster, spattered with its own blood, smacked the weapon out of her hands and scooped her up. Chen dangled in the air, suspended by her right arm in an unbreakable grip.

Charlie had to stop firing in case she hit her friend. Chen drew her sword and fumbled, dropping it. Twisting to draw her pistol left-handed, she shot the creature point-blank in the head. It shrieked and bit down. Chen screamed in agony. Walker ran into the light, arms waving like windmills. The creature dropped the Chinese woman and tried to grab the robot. Chen hit the floor hard and crumpled, holding a mangled hand to her chest. Charlie opened fire and the giant charged at her. She ran, sprinting out along the nearest hallway. Without her light and in the absence of gunfire, the entrance hall went black.

But not completely. Gath saw his pistol over by the doors, its light still working. Getting to his feet, he staggered towards it, his back on fire. There was another tooth-rattling roar and a dull clank. Walker skidded across the tiles in a shower of sparks. Throwing himself towards the weapon, Gath rolled and came up with the pistol pointed straight at the monster. His weapon light caught the face inside the hood. Skin hung in flaps below a distended maw. Button eyes fixed on him as lips peeled back over too many teeth. The fucker was smiling.

It stomped forward and Gath fired until the weapon slide locked back. The thing bore down on him, in no hurry to rip the little man to pieces. Shots rang out from the other end of the hall. The hammering of Charlie's submachine gun. Shots whizzed by, punching holes in the double doors, letting in chinks of light. As sunlight fell on the creature, it screeched in pain, holding up a massive hand. Gath reloaded and started firing as fast as he could. Not at the beast, but at the doors. Panes broke apart and light poured in. The creature howled and started running, back through the hall, into the shadows.

Gath found himself on the floor, but he couldn't remember falling. He lay flat, ignoring the broken glass.

"Chen!" someone called.

It was Charlie. Walker appeared from nowhere carrying Lang, his clothing torn and some of his metal structure exposed. Charlie moved out of the darkness half-dragging Chen. She pushed the doors open and went out into the light. Gath staggered to the doorway and gripped the frame, breathing hard. Laying Chen at the top of the steps, Charlie worked on her hand. Two fingers were gone and the rest was a mess, so Charlie dressed the wound, giving her a handful of painkillers. She couldn't risk anything stronger until they were safe. Chen moaned, eyes shut, shivering. Charlie held her and gently stroked her face.

"You're fine, you're all fixed up, it's OK."

Chen dribbled tears and snot down her face, talking in Chinese. Gath limped back into the entrance hall and gathered Chen's weapons. The fight had burned through most of their ammo. They could use the frangible PIKE rounds against the infected but needed normal loads for Lexington. He looked into the darkness. There was no sign of the creature coming back with the door open, but he kept a wary eye out anyway. Chen's sword and pistol went in his pack, the submachine gun over his shoulder so he could keep an eye on the Merson. The contact warning had come too late, but it had still come. Chen was sitting up when he emerged.

"I can take it," she said, pointing at the SMG.

Gath handed the weapon over.

"I guess we're going to the hospital after all," said Lang.

Charlie gave her a withering look as they pulled on their masks and goggles and then cinched their hoods into place. Charlie had to help Chen do the same while Gath tied his old scarf around Lang's face. He slapped Walker on the shoulder.

"You did great. I'm making you an honorary human."

The robot swiveled its head to look at him.

"Take Dr. Lang to the Matvee."

The machine moved down the steps and headed towards the football field. The rest followed at Chen's beleaguered pace.

"What was it?" asked Charlie as they walked.

"I don't know," said Gath. "I pissed myself."

"It's still back there. Still alive."

"It won't go into the light."

"What happens when it gets dark?"

Gath had no answer. He needed a drink. They trudged on through the snow. It didn't take long to get back to the M-ATV. Gath moved around to the front and popped the hood. Inside it was more like a giant lawnmower, but he had worked on his share of electric engines. The inverter had been knocked loose by the crash, so he reconnected it. It didn't take them long to get the vehicle running and out of the hole. Gath didn't enjoy dragging Erlich's body out of the front seat, but he did it as respectfully as he could.

"I need her clothes," said Lang.

"They're covered in blood."

"I don't care, it's cold."

It took Gath and Charlie a full five minutes to peel the parka and the pants from the body. With an unspoken apology, he dropped the dead soldier into the pit.

"Get in, I'll open the back."

Climbing into the rear, Gath found the release for the back hatches. They opened up on hydraulics and steps descended. Gath and Charlie lifted Lang into the back and laid her on the left row of seats.

"Thank fuck," said Lang. "I didn't want Westworld carrying me through the streets."

Walker climbed in, stooping awkwardly, then sat. Gath closed the back and moved through to the driver's seat.

"Where to?"

"Medstar, the university hospital," said Lang. "Just down the road."

"I might need directions."

"Someone help me into this parka," said Lang. "I'm freezing my tits off."

Chapter 19

"John sent you."

Lang propped herself up on one arm as she lay in the back. It wasn't a question, but Gath answered it anyway.

"Yes."

He didn't turn around. The road ahead was clogged with snow and wreckage. Progress was slow but even at a crawl, his passengers were getting banged about. Charlie made sure Chen and Lang were strapped in. Walker gripped a steel rail.

"He asked me to give you something," Gath went on, "a vial."

"Where is it?"

"It's safe."

Lang lapsed into silence and Gath focused on driving. It wasn't easy over this terrain, but the seat was comfortable, and the heating was on. He tried to relax. There would be precious little downtime when they arrived. Charlie was right, hospitals were ground zero. Any place the sick were in the dying days of December would be infested. But there was no choice. Chen and Lang could die without the right drugs, and he wasn't going to let that happen.

"Why didn't John send special forces?" asked Lang.

Gath kept his eyes on the road. "We saved your life, that's special enough."

"I'd still like a SEAL team. If you're not SF, what are you?"

"Two astronauts and a Fed."

"No prizes for guessing who's the Fed."

"Maybe we should take you back to the showers," said Charlie.

Lang ignored her. "Where's John?"

Gath hesitated. "He's dead. I'm sorry."

Lang lay back down and closed her eyes. Gath nearly missed the turnoff and gave a sharp twist of the wheel. The hospital access road was blocked by abandoned cars and ambulances. Maneuvering around the worst of it, Gath edged between two SUVs and rolled over a Corvette. They could see the hospital complex ahead, like a red brick prison, six stories high. A sign on the right said *Entrance 1, Georgetown University Hospital, MedStar Health*. There was a list of departments below, but only the first interested Gath. *Emergency*. There was an arrow pointing straight ahead and he brought the big vehicle to a halt.

"What's wrong?" asked Charlie.

"I'm thinking."

Lang cleared her throat. "Tick-tock."

If they parked too close to the ER, they could be swamped by infected before they could escape. Things seemed peaceful, but that could change. He tapped the CROWS turret controls. The system was an upgrade, but nothing he couldn't handle. There was an answering rumble from the roof.

"I might need the turret, it'll be loud."

"We ran out of bullets," said Lang.

Gath peered at the icons and saw one blinking red. He switched it off.

"We're on the final approach to the ER. If there are too many infected, I'll have to get us out fast. Brace yourselves."

They started moving again towards the Patient Drop-off Point. Gath drank in the details, his eyes everywhere, ready to slam into reverse at the first sign of trouble. Movement on the left, a plastic bag, skittering across the snow. They rolled on, approaching the covered drop-off point. The ER was fronted in dark-tinted glass. Gath braked 30 yards away and cut the engine.

"Drive up to the doors," said Charlie.

"I want to keep the Matvee back. If they come through the glass, we'll need somewhere to run. Open the hatch."

Charlie yanked the left hatch lever and they helped lift Lang out and settle her in Walker's arms.

"Keep it quiet," said Gath. "No way to know what's in there, but there's got to be infected. Straight in, straight out."

"Not straight out," said Lang. "We need to be sedated. 12 hours."

Gath shook his head and drew his pistol. "Right. We'll want somewhere we can defend."

He headed toward the entrance. Chen was suffering, her movements sluggish. They came to a set of sliding glass doors. Gath reached out and wiped away a layer of frost. Inside was empty, with nothing of the chaos he would have expected at the end. Pulling off his gloves, he pressed the tips of his fingers into the seam where the doors met. He couldn't get a grip. Unclipping his knife, he slid it into the rubber to carve out hand-holds high and low.

"Pull the bottom part," he told Charlie.

He put his gloves back on and they tried the doors, inching them open.

Charlie gave a thumbs up. "That's enough."

"A little more."

"I don't have a beer belly."

As she took off her pack, Gath lifted his ski mask and stuck his head through the opening. Smelled of dust and floor cleaner, nothing else. Charlie squeezed inside. Her weapon light swept the reception area, then she disappeared to the left. The doors rolled back.

"Looks like it hasn't been used," said Charlie. "Maybe it was closed."

Daylight oozed through the polarized glass, casting the place in shadow. A long desk ran opposite the doors. *Reception – Emergencies Only*. Rows of green plastic chairs filled the rest of the room, with vending machines, trash cans, and TVs at intervals along the wall. Where it wasn't dim it was dark. They pulled back their hoods and took off the masks and goggles.

Gath put his headgear into a pocket. "These things are itchy."

"Like crabs," said Charlie.

He gave her a look, then switched on his weapon's tactical light.

Lang cleared her throat. "Second Floor."

Gath led them through the seating area towards stairs at the far end. He paused as his light fell on a body slumped beside a Coke machine. A young woman in a red vest with *Need directions? I can help!* printed on it. Her sleeves were rolled up, and her arms were covered in dried blood. Scissors lay in her lap. He went up the steps two at a time. They were on a landing with four sets of swing doors and two elevators. Gath pushed through a door labeled *Triage 1*. Inside were five neat beds with privacy curtains drawn back. Equipment was in glass-fronted cabinets and on carts against the wall. IV stands were gathered in one corner. Another set of swing doors said *Surgery Center*.

"Tell the Terminator to put me down and get a cart, " said Lang.

Without waiting to be told, Walker laid the scientist on the center bed. Charlie and Gath took off their packs and helped Chen with hers.

"I told you to get a cart," said Lang, her breathing labored.

"Wait," said Charlie.

"If you don't do what I say when I say it, someone could die."

"I said fucking wait."

After they helped Chen into the next bed, Charlie grabbed a cart and wheeled it over to Lang.

"Get two IV bags from that cabinet and two stands," said the scientist, her voice weaker than before. "Two bottles of sterile solution, two saline flushes, a box of alcohol wipes, and four 10cc syringes with needles. Those ones."

Lang continued to rattle off items and Charlie moved around the room, filling the cart. Gath didn't know what half the things were but Charlie seemed to.

"Your friend needs a broad-spectrum intravenous antibiotic, anything with cilastatin or meropenem on it. If you can't find those, I'll tell you more."

Charlie grabbed a bottle. "It's powder."

"It dissolves in saline. Now listen, this is the complicated part."

Gath pushed through the doors to the Surgery Center. A corridor ran north passed a washroom and an upended linen cart. Sheets spilled out over the tiles, bright and clean. There was another set of double doors at the end of the corridor. Gath made sure the washroom was empty before taking the opportunity to piss. He threw cool water onto his face and stared into the mirror. Old and tired. Gath made his way back to Triage 1. Charlie was mixing solutions for Lang and Chen was asleep.

"Go downstairs," he told Walker. "Guard the Matvee."

The machine turned on the spot and went back through the doors to the stairs. Gath watched as Lang guided Charlie through the preparations as if she did it every day, pink notebook in her lap. IV bags were set up for both patients, needles went into their arms.

"Now inject the benzodiazepine into the IV."

"That's a sedative," said Gath.

Lang glanced at him. "Smart boy."

"Do Chen, but not Dr. Lang."

The scientist glared at him. "David, are you trying to fuck me? You're trying to fuck me. We had an agreement."

"We still have an agreement."

"But you're going to fuck me anyway."

"I want a few answers before you're sedated."

Charlie injected Chen's IV, then dropped the syringe into the trash. She leaned against the wall and folded her arms.

Lang scowled. "I shouldn't have trusted you."

"You can trust me. Just a few questions."

"Fine, I'll start. Who murdered John?"

"I didn't say he was murdered."

"Who did it?"

Gath let out a breath. "One of the crew. Carter."

"I want you to kill him."

"I'll kill him, but not for you. My turn." Gath took a shiny metal tube from his pouch. "What's this?"

"I guess it's the vial you're supposed to give me."

"It's not a guess, is it? You know what it is because John told you. He kept in contact with you all along."

Lang looked down at her notebook.

Gath went on. "You asked which crew member like you knew us. Not from TV, but because John told you."

"David Gath, Air Force Colonel, two tours in Iraq and Afghanistan," said Lang. "Divorced. Wife cheated on him more than once. Likes to drink. Loser."

Gath watched as she picked up a bottle of water from the cart and took a sip.

"Yes, John told me. You were told to bring four vials, not one. Where are the rest?"

"Is it a cure?"

"There is no cure. You can't cure prion disease. The vial contains a vaccine precursor. Right now, it isn't anything. When I finish it, it'll make people immune."

Charlie's hands were balled into fists. "My friend was bitten. I could've saved her."

"No, you couldn't."

"You don't know that."

"I do know, honey, because I'm an expert. It's my business to know. Don't you listen? There is no cure. Once you're infected, that's it, game over."

Charlie was pale with anger. She looked like she was going to say something else, then turned away to the window.

"Why did he want you to have it?" asked Gath. "Why not the CDC?"

"Because I'm the best."

"Better than Nobel Prize winners?"

"The best work's done in secret. We don't get prizes."

"If it's secret, how did John know?"

Lang shrugged. "We were fucking. Maybe it was more than fucking. He knows how good I am. Knew."

"Why did John have a vaccine precursor on the space station? He said he was doing private research, but he wasn't, I checked the logs. He never worked on it at all."

The woman stayed silent.

"You said 'when I finish it,'" said Gath, eyes locked on hers. "It wasn't his research, was it? It was yours."

Lang started to speak but coughed instead. Gath passed her the water bottle, and she gulped the liquid down. She kept the bottle in her lap beside her notebook.

"Why were you making a vaccine for a disease no one knew about?"

Lang took another sip of water. "I can tell you, but you won't like it."

"I haven't liked anything in a long time, Doctor."

The scientist pursed her lips, thought for a moment, then gave a slight nod.

"The Pentagon only has one job. To plan. They have plans for everything. Bombing Moscow, invading Canada, little green men. Project Early Light was their plan to defend against a devastating biological attack. To stop the most terrifying disease imaginable. The centerpiece of the plan was a vaccine, but you can't have a vaccine for a disease that doesn't exist. So, they made one. Catakuru Prion. What the media calls White's Disease."

Lang took a long drink of water.

"They asked me to develop the vaccine. John was doing research for the army and I had him transferred to my team. By the time went back to NASA, the vaccine was almost complete."

"What happened?" asked Charlie.

"We were working out of the USAMRIID labs at Fort Detrick."

USAMRIID was the United States Army Medical Research Institute for Infectious Diseases.

"The bomb," said Gath.

"They blew up the lab and murdered my team. If I wasn't late getting back from DC, I'd have been killed too. All the work was gone. No backups."

"But John had a sample."

"I didn't know. He took it to work on while he was away. Son of a bitch."

Gath was trying to put the pieces together.

"Did the bomb release the disease?"

"No, it's bloodborne. A subject needs to be directly contaminated, blood to blood. An injection or a bite. Infected gums bleed, so a bite transmits the pathogen."

"So it was intentionally released?"

"That's the only way. Someone had to deliberately infect patient zero."

"Who?"

"If I knew, I'd be dead. If they can take out Detrick, they can sure as shit get to me."

No one spoke. The silence grew.

"Can I have my sedative now?" asked Lang.

Charlie picked up the syringe and injected the IV.

"If we get you back to Aegis, can you finish your work?" asked Gath.

"Of course."

"Then what?"

"Aegis has the facilities to mass-produce doses." Lang closed her eyes. "If there are any people left."

The scientist sagged into the pillow. Charlie set the empty syringe onto the tray.

"So. We made it."

"We made it but we didn't use it. There's a difference."

"Tell that to the dead."

Charlie sat down on the end of a bed.

"I'm tired," she said.

"I was tired hours ago. Don't think there's a word for what I am now. Let's block the doors, then we can sleep."

"Is there a toilet?"

He pointed to the Surgery Center. "Halfway along the corridor."

She left Gath alone with the unconscious patients. There was so much swirling around in his mind, he didn't know where to start. He was bone weary. All he could think of was sleep. Gath looked at a syringe on the tray. One nice injection and it was lights out for 12 hours. Heaven.

"You're in a world of your own," said Charlie from the door.

"You're a fast pisser."

"Lovely. I guess when you're an astronaut you don't need to sweet talk the girls."

"I was married most of the time."

"Does it matter?"

"It did to me. We need to tie the handles, then block the doors with those cabinets. I can hear the bed calling me."

He grabbed an MRE out of his pack. "You like Blueberry Cobbler?"

She smiled. "I like everything."

"That's the first."

"First what?"

"Smile, in a while."

Charlie said nothing and Gath wished he'd kept his mouth shut. Standing, he picked up some rubber tubing and tied it through the handles of the doors to the Surgery Center. Between them, they maneuvered the nearest cabinet in front of it.

"Give me a second."

Gath massaged his lower back and walked to the window. He put his hands on the sill and rested for a moment. The M-ATV lay below on the access road, Walker standing sentinel beside it. They were on a hill with a decent view of DC. Buildings of every shape and size stretched out to the horizon, all capped in white. It was bright and clear and still. Charlie stood beside him.

"How long do you need to rest, Grandpa?"

"Longer than I've got."

Charlie touched the glass and looked out at the cityscape. "It's beautiful."

Gath thought it looked dead, but he remembered to keep his mouth shut. They stared out at the city together, neither feeling the need to talk.

"You think she can make a vaccine?" asked Charlie.

"I don't know what to think."

"Will it make any difference?"

Gath wanted to hug her but he didn't know how.

The explosion struck without warning. Gath was slammed back by the shockwave before he heard the boom. He hit the bed and rolled onto the floor. There was a ringing and he tasted blood. Charlie groaned nearby. It was an attack. Gath groped for Chen's submachine gun in the broken glass and crawled under the window. Charlie slid across to join him. They inched up to look out where the window used to be. The M-ATV was burning, smoke pouring from the wreckage. Walker lay a few yards away. At the bottom of the access road, eight figures in black bodysuits and Kevlar skimmed across the snow on silent motorbikes.

"Lexington," said Gath.

"What are they riding?"

The machines looked like white Skidoos, but sleeker. a ski runner on the front and a wide off-trail track at the rear.

"Snow Bikes," said Gath. "Fast but hard to handle."

Gath unclipped his binoculars and brought them up. Lexington came to a halt. They carried pistols in shoulder holsters. One carried an anti-tank weapon slung across his back. Charlie pulled the charging handle on her submachine gun.

"What are we going to do?"

"Fight. We can't run and can't surrender. We need to kill as many as we can before they get to the hospital. PIKE rounds won't get passed their armor, so we've only one magazine each of normal SMG ammo. After that, it's pistols."

"The explosion will bring the infected."

"Not fast enough. We'll open up at 50 yards."

The mercenaries dismounted and continued on foot in a staggered line. Gath put his binoculars away and extended the metal stock on his SMG.

"Wait until they get to the Bronco."

It was a long minute before Lexington reached the SUV. Gath and Charlie opened fire at once, emptying their magazines in a few seconds. Three enemies were down, including the one with the anti-tank weapon. The rest scattered, hiding behind the Bronco or dropping to the snow. Gath and Charlie crouched and drew pistols.

"They'll fire at us while they re-position," said Gath. "Close your eyes."

Bullets hit the ceiling and the window frame. The shots were suppressed so the only sound was the impact. Gath and Charlie fired back and then hid again to reload.

"Get any?" asked Charlie.

"No. One of the bodies is gone, so six left. We'll hit them when they come up the stairs."

"What if they come the other way?"

"We lose."

The Surgery Center doors were tied shut and blocked by a cabinet. If they came that way, it might delay them.

They didn't have enough firepower to stop an attack from both directions. Gath divided up the remaining .45 ammunition.

"Grab those test tubes," he told Charlie.

Gath picked up a box of glass beakers and they moved through the swing doors. The stairs were bordered on three sides by a four-foot safety wall of painted concrete. Gath emptied his beakers and Charlie's test tubes down the steps. They smashed into tiny pieces, spilling across the tiles on the floor below.

"We'll be playing by ear. If you hear glass crunch, start shooting."

"What are our chances?"

"Not good."

"You need to learn how to lie."

Chapter 20

They were coming. Gath focused on what he could hear above the pounding of his heart. He imagined a squad of mercenaries creeping up on them. It wasn't real, but it would be. Lexington would kill them all for the vial. Gath didn't want to die. Something clattered, back toward the entrance downstairs, far enough away to risk a quick peek. It was an old trick, but Gath was an old dog. The enemy made a noise to misdirect, to get the defenders to give away their position. That meant the bastards were close, very close. Gath gave Charlie a hand signal, telling her to stay in cover and hold fire.

A scuffing sound came from the bottom of the steps and Gath blinked away sweat. It was cold in the stairwell but he still felt hot. The stairs were an obvious chokepoint and experienced soldiers would approach with caution. When they saw the broken glass they would know the second floor was defended. They could storm it or find another way up. With no time to find a new route, they would try a frontal assault. A grenade would have ended things quickly, but they couldn't risk the vial. Gath strained to hear movement, but these guys were good. If he didn't know better, he might think no one was near. But he did know better.

Charlie reared up and fired over the wall. Time slowed as Gath surged to his feet. He saw everything. A *Do Not Run* sign under peeling plastic, worn patches on the handrail, the cheap off-white paint on the plaster walls. There wasn't a squad of Lexington operatives, only two. One was already falling, blood spraying out from the hole Charlie put in his head. The second attacker was close enough to touch, turning away to shoot Charlie. Gath fired point-blank, and the man's hooded head cracked like an egg. Both mercenaries slid to the bottom, leaving smears of blood on the steps. They came to rest side by side on the tiled floor like it was planned that way.

There was a crack from behind and Charlie staggered. She was confused, a stain spreading on her collar. Dropping the pistol she grabbed the wall, then fell back. Gath ran to her and knelt, terrified. He peeled back the top of her jacket; blood was everywhere. Covering the wound in her neck, he couldn't remember how much pressure to apply. Charlie grabbed his arm and looked at him without knowing. Her mouth moved like she wanted to speak, then her hand dropped away. Gath shouted something and held her tight. All he could hear was roaring.

"Get up!" someone shouted.

Gath closed his eyes and started rocking the body. They hit him, but it didn't hurt. His arms were wrenched back and he was hauled to his feet. They dragged him into the triage room and dropped him in a heap. Two mercenaries stood over him, one had a bandaged shoulder. Lang and Chen still lay unconscious in bed. The Surgery Center doors had been forced, the cabinet pushed back. Lexington had come from two directions at once. Gath wiped blood from his face. He didn't know if it was his or Charlie's.

"Did you search him?" asked one of the mercenaries. It was a woman.

The wounded man held out the metal vial. "There's a computer too."

"Don't care about computers."

She took the vial. Gath didn't remember being searched. Another mercenary opened the Surgery Center doors, the right side banging into the cabinet.

"Glad you could make it, Pell," snapped the woman.

Pell moved the cabinet out of the way. The female mercenary pointed to the backpacks.

"Make yourself useful, check their gear."

Pell nodded and started unzipping packs, rifling through the contents. A fourth mercenary came in from the stairs. He didn't speak and moved to the beds, checking Lang and Chen, lifting the bandages to get a better look. He picked up Lang's notebook and thumbed through the pages. Gath watched from the floor, wanting to fight and be sick at the same time but doing neither. He was kneeling but he didn't know why. All his strength had drained away. The man tucked the notebook into his Kevlar vest and crouched in front of Gath, pulling off his hood. He was in his 30s, fit and handsome.

"How come slick guys on seven-figure salaries can make artificial gravity but can't make coffee?"

Ethan Carter was a traitor. He had been a crew member on the space station and a friend, but now he was nothing.

"I have to admit, old-timer, I was expecting more," said Carter. "How did you know it was me?"

Gath reached into a pouch and produced a small tool embossed with a rocket ship.

Carter took it. "Wondered where I left that."

The tool was unique and proved that Carter had betrayed them. He turned to look at the woman.

"Bless, dear."

The woman handed him the vial. He held it up in front of Gath.

"This was harder than it needed to be." He put it into a pouch. "You found Dr. Lang, but she's infected."

Gath shook his head slightly.

"I saw the bites," said Carter. "Doesn't matter. I've got her notebook, don't need her. Sad about Chen, but no one's going to miss the good doctor."

Bless drew her weapon and aimed it at Lang.

"Wait," said Gath. "They're not infected."

"They were bitten."

"Not by the infected."

"What by?"

"A thing."

"A thing?"

"I don't know."

"You're not making much sense, Dave."

Gath swallowed. "They're not infected. Look at Lang. The bites are old."

Carter mulled it over then nodded at Bless, who lowered her pistol. He stood.

"The lovely Bless is coming with me back to base. Unlovely Kinsey and Pell, you're staying here until the helicopter comes. If the women turn, shoot them."

"Why do I have to stay? I'm wounded," said Kinsey.

"Because you're an idiot." Carter grinned at Gath. "See you, old-timer. When you're back, Sobek wants a word, then you and me can have a good chinwag."

Sobek was the head of Lexington. Gath wasn't eager for a reunion. He wanted to say something, to hurt Carter, but no words came. The younger man pulled on his hood, the slick material tight against his skin, and strapped on goggles.

"The infected are coming, Kinsey. Don't fuck this up."

He left with Bless, the doors swinging closed.

"That guy is one massive gaping asshole," said Kinsey. He looked at Gath. "Was he always a dick?"

Gath's face was blank and the mercenary walked to the window.

"Fuck, they're everywhere." He produced a handful of zip-ties. "I told him no explosions, but he never damn well listens." He turned to Pell. "We need to lock down. I'll close the doors, you move the cabinets."

Kinsey ran across to the Surgery Center exit and started tying the door handles. Pell walked towards the cabinet, then changed direction, coming up behind the other mercenary. He grabbed Kinsey's head, wrenching it back, and rammed a knife into the man's neck. The mercenary thrashed a few times, then went limp. Pell dropped the body and wiped his blade on the sheets of the nearest bed. Sheathing his knife, the man took off his hood. Except it wasn't a man.

"Ahoy sailor," said Remikov.

It was a dead woman. Maria Remikov died six days ago. The Russian moved passed the beds and started moving the cabinet back to the door. Gath gaped at her.

"Help me," she said.

Gath managed to get to his feet and join her, dragging the cabinet back into position against the Surgery Center doors. If he wasn't surprised when Carter took off his hood, he was astonished to see Remikov. She bent over and searched Kinsey's body, holding up a pistol and extra magazines.

Gath was still staring. "You're alive."

"Take this, we have to go."

He took the weapon and ammunition.

"I can't believe it."

"We can talk later," said Remikov. "The infected are coming. Help me with the other one."

Together they wrestled the second cabinet out of the swing doors. When they stood on the landing by the stairs, Remikov tied the handles and they maneuvered the cabinet into position.

"That should keep them safe until we get back," said the woman, replacing her headgear. "We're going outside, do you have a face covering?"

"Why?"

"We have to stop Carter."

Gath couldn't even look at Charlie's body as they went down the stairs. He did his best to keep up as Remikov broke into a jog. They ran through reception and out of the open doors. Smoke billowed from the wreckage of the M-ATV, it was everywhere, infected milling around in the haze. Gath pulled on his ski mask and goggles against the cold. Remikov went first, firing at shapes that came too close. Gath found Walker on the ground, shredded and singed, his arm missing. It was a pity. The robot had become a kind of friend. Remikov killed infected as they appeared, never using more than one shot. Gath didn't even need to draw his pistol.

The smoke thinned and they saw the parked Snow Bikes. In the distance, Carter and Bless were on two more, turning east into the city.

"Can you drive those bikes?" asked Remikov.

"I can drive anything."

They passed an ambulance and an infected lunged at Gath. He had time to see an EMT uniform and a fleshless face before the top of the man's head came off. Instead of falling, the thing snarled at Remikov, who shot him again. Nothing else got close before they made it to the bikes. Keys were in the ignition, so Gath swung his leg over and started it. Remikov pulled away almost immediately and he hit the accelerator. The bike was faster than he remembered and he drew level.

They raced across the snow, swerving to avoid cars and the infected. Turning out of the access road, they caught sight of Carter and Bless, moving at a leisurely pace in the distance. Remikov sped up as fast as she dared and he took up position on her right. They needed to close the gap before the others spotted them. Gath zigged around a burned-out SUV and powered ahead. He had a pistol but he couldn't shoot and steer at the same time. Soon the whine of the electric bikes would be unmissable, even with the wind. Ramming was a possibility, but at these speeds, he would break his neck.

Remikov swerved to avoid a truck and raced along the sidewalk. There was a square with trees, statues, and benches at the end of the avenue. Bless looked over one shoulder and shouted a warning. She and Carter immediately accelerated, jinking to the left, down a narrow street lined with two-story houses. Remikov gunned her engine, cutting through a bus stop, and running up the back of a Volkswagen Beetle almost buried in snow. The Russian shot off the roof of the car, landing on the road 20 yards ahead. There was no way Gath could match that. Remikov drew her pistol and started firing, in full control of her machine.

The mercenaries decided to split up, heading in opposite directions. Remikov took off after Bless so it was up to Gath to stop Carter. Pushing the engine hard, he jerked the handlebars at the last second and nearly fell off. Flooring the accelerator, he shot down a side street. If he didn't take more risks he was never going to catch up. He couldn't live with Carter getting away. Making a hard left, the bike skidded too close to a burned-out truck before momentum snatched him away. Swerving right, he saw a Snow Bike lying in the middle of the street. Carter was gone.

There was a sharp crack and Gath flew over the handlebars. He sailed through the air and landed in a drift that covered him completely. Scrambling out he ducked around the corner. Gath found himself outside an office block. He shook his head to clear it and ran to a ramp leading to an underground parking lot. He ran down, slipping on the ice and falling. Lying there for a second, he gathered his wits, then pushed himself up. The place was dim and smelled of oil. Windows lined the top of one wall, letting in a little light from street level.

The parking lot could probably fit 20 cars but there were only a few. Gath moved behind the nearest, a red convertible, foreign, and slid to the ground. He tapped the location tab on GRACE. He was on Suter Lane, an Exxon station at one end of the street, a TD bank at the other. He stuck his head out. Too close to the ramp. Using the last of his energy, he got up and jogged to a white Jeep Avenger toward the back and slumped down. Dog-tired, he waited.

Gath's eyes snapped open, heart hammering. How long had he been asleep? He checked GRACE. A half hour. Shit. There was a noise, over by the entrance. Someone was walking down the ramp and not trying to hide.

"He's gone," said Remikov.

Relief washed over him, but he didn't say anything, trying to order his thoughts.

"Are you awake?"

He heaved himself up. "Of course I'm awake."

Gath hobbled into the open. He felt a bit better for the rest.

"How did you know where I was?"

"You blocked the light."

They walked back up the ramp.

"I lost him," he said.

"I know."

They rounded the corner and saw Gath's bike, bent wreckage now against a pickup truck. Remikov's sat nearby.

"He shot the engine," said Gath, breathing hard.

"I left the woman back at the intersection. 20 minutes' walk. The bikes don't take two. You ride."

"It's your bike."

"You ride."

"Is that because I'm too old or too slow?"

"Yes."

Gath got onto her machine.

"Seems ungallant."

"What does that mean?"

"A bad thing for a man to do to a woman."

"Most things men do to women are bad. Go."

He felt the machine thrum as he switched on the ignition. He set off at a gentle pace, Remikov at his side, making her way easily through the snow. Whether he liked it or not, he was in no shape to walk. They cut along a street

Gath didn't recognize and crossed a wide avenue with old-fashioned street lamps.

"I'm sorry we left you," he said after a while.

Remikov had been on Gath's team when they landed at Port Arthur. They had been attacked by infected at a truck stop on the road to Houston. Gath thought Remikov had been killed.

"You didn't leave me," said the Russian, "I left you. It took most of the night to get away from the infected."

"We hid in a construction yard until morning. Laura didn't make it."

"I found her body. I followed you to Aegis Laboratories. One of these mercenaries tried to stop me. He told me about Lexington and Carter, that they were hunting you. I looked for you in Washington."

Gath wondered what she did to the man to get him to talk. "How did you survive?"

"I'm used to the cold. I found Lexington and followed them to the hospital."

She made it sound easy. They arrived at the intersection to see Bless tied to one of the trees that lined the street. Her arms were zip-tied behind her around the trunk. Bless's head came up.

"Let me go, you cunt!"

Gath held up a hand. "Where's your base?"

"Fuck you, faggot."

Remikov ripped off the woman's hood. Blass was young and black, her head freshly shaved.

"You're not going to last long out here," said Gath.

Bless spat at him.

"You going to die for Carter? I can't see him dying for you."

"Suck a dick, faggot."

Remikov drew the knife she had used on Kinsey. It still had the man's blood on it.

"You going to cut me, bitch?" asked Bless.

Gath was about to tell Remikov to put it away until he remembered Charlie. He moved back to give the Russian room.

Bless struggled against the zip-ties. "I'll show you how to fucking cut, you fucking dyke."

Remikov moved around the tree and pulled off one of Bless's gloves. The mercenary started squirming, clenching and unclenching her fists.

"Where's your base?" asked Gath.

"I'll take that bitch's knife and shove it up your ass. You'll love it."

Bless screamed. Remikov threw a pinky finger into the snow.

"How old are you?"

Bless gritted her teeth and groaned.

"You're a tough kid, but life's a lot better with fingers. Where is your base?"

"Go fuck yourself," she said, spit dribbling down her chin.

She screamed again. Remikov tossed another finger away. Bless shuddered and tears ran down her face, though she made no noise.

"Where's your base?" asked Gath. "The infected are coming. You won't last long tied to a tree."

"Keep cutting, whore." The mercenary's throat was hoarse. "I'm not saying shit."

The Russian cut off Bless's index finger and waved it in front of the shrieking woman's face. After a while, she fell silent, slumped against the tree. Remikov slapped her across the face.

"Tell me," said Gath. "Tell me and I'll take you back to the hospital, patch you up."

"I killed your bitch," said Bless. "Shot her in the throat. It was funny. I laughed."

Gath took the knife from Remikov and moved close to Bless. The mercenary spat blood at him. He grabbed her head and lifted the knife close to her right eye. Without pausing, he jammed it in.

"White House!" shouted Bless, "it's in the White House!"

The knife had slid a half-inch into the bottom of the eyesocket, below the eye. Blood welled up.

"The White House is gone," said Gath.

"There's a bunker under the West Wing."

"If you're lying, I'll blind you."

"It's not a lie. Elevator's got a retinal scan. You need me. I need my eye."

Gath pulled the knife out and blood flowed down Bless's cheek.

"GRACE, bring up the route from Georgetown University Hospital to Suter Lane, then on to the White House."

Suter Lane was where Carter ambushed him. GRACE complied and a blue line ran across a map on the screen. It was nearly a straight line from the hospital, through Suter Lane, to the White House. He threw Remikov the knife.

"Cut her down."

"I don't trust her."

"We're not bringing her with us," said Gath, turning to look at Bless. "We just need her eyes."

Chapter 21

"No guards. I don't like it."

Gath's voice sounded different through the mouth filter. They both wore Lexington bodysuits and armor now. The one Gath took from Bless was a tight fit, but it would do. Lying on top of a tank in Jackson Place, they scanned the perimeter of the West Wing. The White House Residence was gone. All that remained were charred pillars sticking up through the snow.

"Perhaps they are inside," said Remikov. "Or hiding."

"Hiding from who? There isn't anybody else."

Remikov slid off the turret. "Let's go."

They climbed down the side and moved to the bikes.

"Which way?" asked Gath as he got on.

"Through the front door. We are wearing their uniform."

"What happens when we don't answer comms?"

The Russian swung a long leg over her bike. "Where is your sense of adventure, David?"

"I lose it when people try to kill me."

They rode along the line of tanks until they reached a checkpoint. Skirting the red and white barrier, they rode out onto an empty Pennsylvania Avenue. The White House gates were closed, but there were plenty of gaps in the black metal fence. Negotiating concrete barriers and burned-out vehicles, they headed up the driveway to the West Wing. Clouds gathered overhead and Gath tried not to see it as an omen. If a sniper was going to pick him off, there wasn't much he could do about it. There was a clutch of other Snow Bikes under the portico to the left of the doors, so they pulled up beside them and dismounted.

The entrance was marred by scorch marks, but the windows were unbroken. Both doors were pushed back a few inches and it was dark inside.

Gath put his hand on Remikov's arm. "If I get shot, I'm blaming you."

Remikov stood to one side and slowly pushed the doors open. "Nietzsche said what doesn't kill you makes you stronger."

"Nietzsche's dead."

He followed her in and flicked on his weapon light. The richly carpeted hallway had side tables, busts, and vases with dead flowers. They edged along until they entered a small lobby. Paintings hung on the cream-colored walls and armchairs flanked a glass-fronted cabinet. There was a body on the floor behind the mahogany reception desk. Lexington. Remikov crouched down.

"Shot. Back of the head."

"He's killing his own people."

"We don't know who did it." She stood. "Have you been to the Oval Office before?"

"A long time ago, under Obama."

Remikov ran her weapon light along the walls. There were two exits.

"Left or right."

Gath moved to the left door and opened it to reveal a long corridor. The Russian moved ahead to the end, listened at the door, then tried the handle. A wide carpeted hall. Gath shone his light along the oil paintings and antiques on display tables. The hall turned right into rows of small, glass-fronted offices. They moved to the door at the end.

"Did you meet him?" asked Remikov.

"Who?"

"Obama."

"Briefly."

"What did you say?"

He shrugged. "Hello."

They stopped at the door and Remikov put her ear to a wooded panel.

"You meet your President and you only say hello?"

"What was I supposed to say? Never start a land war in Asia?"

"I'm Russian, all of our land wars are in Asia."

Remikov opened the door and shone her light into a long room with blue walls filled with seats. There was a wooden lectern on a podium, two US flags on poles either side.

"Press briefing room," said Gath. "Wrong way."

They backtracked.

"We have a White House in Russia," said Remikov, "but it's for the Prime Minister. The President lives in the Kremlin."

"And you've met Putin."

"Yes."

"More than once."

"Yes."

They came to an elegant dark lacquered door. Gath listened and heard nothing. Inside was large and bright with a wall of French windows. It was dominated by an elliptical mahogany table ringed by leather chairs. There was a large painting of men in 18th Century clothes above the fireplace.

"What is this picture?" asked Remikov.

"Declaration of Independence."

"How do you know?"

"It's famous. This is the Cabinet Room, so we're getting close."

They moved on and Gath's light picked out a door ahead set into a curved wall. Had to be the Oval Office. He tried the handle, but it was locked.

"I can break it," said Remikov.

"Do you go around breaking things in the Kremlin?"

"The Kremlin complex has five palaces and four cathedrals. No one would notice."

"Let's see if there's another way."

Gath moved to a nearby door and entered a small office with two desks. The door opposite was unusual, recessed at an angle.

"This is the Outer Office. Through that door's the Oval."

Photos dotted the desks: family snaps, a smiling woman with the President. Remikov's light found something on the carpet.

"Blood."

Gath swept his light under the desk and saw more dried blood and a shoe.

"What did you say to Putin?" asked Gath. "The last time you met him."

Remikov moved over to the recessed door and listened.

"I said 'There were no survivors, Mr. President'."

She walked into the Oval Office. Inside was bright, the sun streaming in through three large windows behind the Resolute Desk. There were bronze busts, paintings, a marble fireplace, and cream-colored couches. The center of the room was covered by a giant circular blue carpet embroidered with an eagle. Another Lexington mercenary lay face down. Remikov checked the rest of the room before kneeling and removing the dead man's hood. His short blond hair was matted with dried blood.

"Same."

"Now we know why there are no guards," said Gath.

He walked around the desk and looked for a button. They had worked on Bless for as much detail as she could remember before patching up her hand and leaving her hog-tied in a house nearby. Gath found three buttons and pressed them one at a time. The third opened a door in the far wall a few inches. Red light bled out through the gap.

"I'll be back," said Gath, moving to a different door and opening it.

"Where are you going?"

"To the little boy's room."

The only unusual thing about his previous visit to the Oval Office was using the toilet. He had been in the room with the Chief of Staff before the President arrived, and he really needed to go. It was dark in the hallway so he used his light to orient himself. He found a well-appointed study and a modest dining room with a round table and four lacquered chairs. There were saucers and cups set out, dried coffee in the bottom. He opened a door on his right and found the washroom. It took him a while to figure out how to get the bodysuit off so he could piss. The relief was immense. When he returned to the Oval, Remikov was standing in the opened door, framed in red light.

"How is your little boy?" she asked.

"Much better."

Remikov led the way to the end of a metal corridor and down steps to a square room with a single elevator. The Seal of the President glowed red on the control panel.

"GRACE, use the retinal scan."

They had recorded Bless's retinal print. GRACE's screen showed a map of blood vessels from her eye and the seal went blue. The elevator doors opened. It was big enough for ten people inside, with wood paneling and muted lighting. They walked in and the doors closed. There were no buttons, but Gath guessed there didn't need to be. They started going down.

"This is going smoother than I thought," said Gath.

The lights changed to red and they came to a sudden halt. A claxon wailed.

"*Warning,*" said a voice from speakers in the ceiling. "*Biological Hazard Alert. Warning.*"

Panels to each side slid up to reveal small rooms. They weren't part of the elevator but caches sunk into the shaft wall. Each room had a rack of five yellow biohazard suits.

"*Warning, Biological Hazard Alert. Please follow Biological Hazard safety procedures. Warning.*"

"What do we do?" shouted Gath over the noise.

Remikov unstrapped her Kevlar body armor, taking off her equipment belt and shoulder holster. She stepped into the left room and started putting on one of the suits. It was a standard civilian model, with biohazard markings and a full-face clear respirator. She began tightening the seals around the boot coverings and the waist then removed the Lexington hood.

"Do as I do," she said.

Gath took the nearest biohazard suit and followed her lead.

"*Warning, Biological Hazard Alert. Please follow Biological Hazard safety procedures. Warning.*"

Remikov and Gath buckled equipment belts and holsters over the suits, put on the respirators, and sealed the hoods. It smelled of rubber inside.

"Warning, Biological Hazard Alert. Warning."

As they moved back into the elevator, the side panels slid back up. The elevator began to move down once more and the claxons stopped. Lights cycled back to soft white. The doors opened onto an empty, brightly lit blue corridor running to a T junction. The wall at the junction bore the Seal of the President of the United States.

"GRACE?"

His voice came through the biohazard suit's external speaker.

"Yes, David?"

"Can you give us any information on the bunker or the biohazard?

"It is a closed system. I detect no controlling artificial intelligence in this facility and there is no interface to access. I see nothing visually on any spectrum to indicate potential biohazard but am unable to conduct testing."

"Invisible, like Sarin gas," said Remikov.

"Or there's nothing there."

He walked to the junction. There was a heavy security door to the right, but the left passageway was open. Gath went to the closed door and examined it. Reinforced steel brushed to a matt finish. It had two thin blue lines across the middle and a series of small stenciled numbers. The access panel was a simple square of dark glass. Gath tapped it, pressed it, and then hit it. Nothing.

"Can you get this open?" he asked.

"No," said Remikov. "We can go the other way."

"We might live longer if we go our own way. GRACE, what kind of lock is this?"

"*A Kaba Mas 212 Security Panel.*"

"How do we open it?"

"*Retinal scan, fingerprint scan, manual code, or by voice recognition, but it has been locked down. There is no way to interface with it. It requires the lockdown to be lifted from a central security hub.*"

The Russian walked the other way.

"Where are you going?"

"Through the open door."

With no alternative, Gath followed. They entered some sort of security area with body scanners, chairs, a desk, a wired wall phone, and a computer. A dead Lexington mercenary lay sprawled face down over the desk. There was a digital readout on the wall; *PEOC 2 SEC 12/H* in green letters.

"PEOC is Presidential Emergency Operations Center," said Gath, "SEC is probably security. Don't know about the numbers."

The way ahead was open, running straight then turning right. Gath tapped on the computer keyboard, but there was no response. Leaning over the corpse, he looked at bullet holes in the suit and Kevlar. It had been shot more than once. The body stank of corruption. Remikov pulled off the rubberized hood. His face was gray, with black lesions across the desiccated skin, eyes like poached eggs.

"Infected, but I can't see a bite."

She took two magazines from the man and handed one to Gath.

"I've enough ammo."

"Take it anyway."

They continued on through into an admin area where everything was bare and utilitarian. No little keepsakes, no photos. The digital readout said *PEOC 41 ADM 9/E.* Entering a mess hall that could fit a hundred, they found only one table that showed signs of use. Four half-finished MREs and a cup on the floor. The food was fresh and it looked like whoever was eating had been interrupted. There were a number of exits but only one was open.

"We're being led down the garden path," said Gath.

Remikov was examining another black-clad body on the floor.

"Infected and shot four times," was her verdict. "No bites."

"How can there be no bites?"

Remikov shrugged. They took the open passage into a large communications room with a digital world map on the wall. There were rows of workstations with padded headsets. Two of the exits were sealed and one was open.

"I really want to stop going through the open doors," said Gath.

Remikov went to one of the sealed exits. There was a viewscreen below the security panel. It showed infected, lots of them, pressing too close. Some were in uniform, Marines in dress blues, and staff officers from different services.

"Are they in the next room?" asked Gath.

"I don't know. I think so. The lockdown is keeping them away."

Gath saw a uniform he recognized, an air force general. Part of his face had been torn away.

"That's Clark Quinn, Central Command."

"A friend?"

"No."

The guy was an ass, but he deserved better than this. Remikov checked the viewscreen on the other exit.

"More in here."

There was a noise behind them. Three Lexington mercenaries hurled themselves through the open door. Instead of firing, they ran forward, arms out like brawlers. They moved like they were in pain. Infected. The nearest swiped at Gath and snarled. Gath shot him in the chest, right into the Kevlar and the man grabbed his arms. As they grappled, the mercenary's head snapped to one side. Gath felt hands grab him from behind and teeth bit into his shoulder. Remikov fired again and Gath broke free. He spun around but all the attackers were dead.

"He bit me," said Gath.

He couldn't believe it. So fast, no time to react. Just like Neet had been infected.

"Where?"

"My shoulder."

Remikov turned him around and inspected his suit. Gath started to shake. Remikov slapped him on the back.

"No bite."

"I felt it."

"There's no bite."

She pointed at the body. It wore the standard Lexington hood.

"The mouth is covered, he couldn't bite through."

Gath took a long breath and looked at another body lying nearby. The man's teeth were visible where he had chewed through the hood.

"If I was bitten, would you shoot me?" asked Gath.

"Yes."

They reloaded and moved on, coming to a junction with two open security doors. Gath examined each doorway in turn.

"I don't like it."

"You didn't like when we had one door. Now there are two."

"I still don't like it."

Remikov said nothing and went left while Gath went right. After a few steps, he heard a noise and turned back. Remikov's door had closed.

"Maria?"

He hit the steel with the butt of his pistol and then pressed the security panel, but it was locked down like the others.

"Maria!" he shouted. "Don't wait for me, find the security hub. I'll do the same."

He knew she probably couldn't hear him but there was no point getting angry. This was someone else's game. The only real chance to win was to find the player and put a bullet in him. Gath continued along a corridor that ran straight then left. He arrived at a four-way junction. Each direction looked the same and there was nothing to indicate which route to take. He went straight and found himself in another security room, with an open door leading out.

"Pick a card, any card."

He looked around for security cameras. Though he couldn't see them, he had no doubt they were there. He hoped Carter was enjoying himself. It wouldn't last long.

Gath came to a medical area. Blood bathed the place, slopped on the beds, and spattered across the screens. Emergency equipment was strewn across the floor. It was a far cry from the cleanliness of the rest of the bunker. A readout on the wall in green said *PEOC 9 MED 14/B*. There were two bodies on beds, covered in stained sheets. Gath lifted the fabric from the first corpse. The woman was long dead. She had been autopsied, the y-shaped scar on her torso not as neat as he had seen in movies.

He checked the other one. There was an ID lanyard hanging on a nearby IV stand. *Samir Saha, Associate Counsel, Office of the White House Counsel.* Most of the flesh on the face was stripped away. Whatever had happened here, it was months ago. Gath took the only exit open and passed through a maintenance area with another Lexington body. Through a store room filled with MREs, he emerged into a rec room with ping pong tables, foosball, arcade machines, and two more bodies.

Gath went through another door and an infected mercenary rushed at him. Gath shot him in the leg and then blew his jaw off. He meant to hit the head the first time, but the heart was beating out of his chest and he missed. The jaw looked like it was enough, and the man lay unmoving on the floor. He was in a corridor lined with chairs along one wall, like a waiting area, with two closed doors. The readout on the wall said *PEOC 1 SIT 1/A*. There was no way forward and worry started to creep in. What if he couldn't get to Remikov? What if he was trapped down here? He checked the suit tank display in his helmet. Six hours of oxygen remained. After that, he would have to sample the air and take his chances.

One of the doors slid open. He could see part of a conference table with black swivel chairs. Gath stepped inside. The room was uncomfortably hot. Papers and tablet computers were strewn between plates, mugs, and bottles of water. Around the walls were hard-wired phones and TV screens showing security footage from the bunker. Carter was in the center seat facing him. His hood was off and he was deathly pale, lesions streaking his face.

"Welcome to the Situation Room."

The door closed.

Though Gath had come to kill him, he was still appalled at the other man's appearance. A couple of hours ago, Carter had been at the peak of physical fitness. Now he looked like just another corpse. He had been infected, and the disease was spreading fast. Gath raised his pistol and Carter laughed.

"You can shoot me later, old-timer."

His voice was dry and cracked. He coughed and brought up black mucous. Carter was about to speak when he coughed again.

"The medulla controls autonomic activity. I'm coughing because the disease is eating into my brain. Knowledge is a wonderful thing, but sometimes it's better not to know."

Carter spat a gobbet of something dark onto the floor then took a drink from a bottle beside him.

"It's in the air."

Gath's weapon never wavered. "White's Disease isn't airborne."

"It is now. It's all through the bunker. I activated the biohazard protocols for you. Wish someone had done the same for me."

Carter tapped a control. The main screen at the end of the table changed to show a video feed of Remikov examining a sealed security door. She was trapped.

"Always had a thing for Maria, " said Carter.

"Let her go."

"After we talk."

Carter was wracked by a bout of coughing and bile trickled down his chin. He poured more water into his mouth, spilling most of it. Gath holstered the pistol. There was no point. A new image flashed on the main screen. It was a close-up of a document. *TOPSECRET// COMINT//ORCON// X1* ran across the top. *NSA/Central Security Service Exceptionally Controlled Information*. NSA was the National Security Agency, a US government intelligence organization.

"Lexington was NSA. A deniable asset for wet work. We killed people who couldn't be brought to trial. Our last target was an anti-government group called the Faction."

A series of images appeared showing dozens of personnel files, long-lense pictures, and drone photos. The people in the pictures were all military officers.

"The Faction was all male, veterans from elite units, special forces, key people in special commands. We took them out, one by one."

An image showed the personnel record of a black army colonel with a chest full of medals.

"John Barnes was too high-profile for normal sanction."

"John loved this country."

"They all loved the country but they hated politicians. We all know the government, stinking the place out like a load of old whores."

Carter coughed again. Fluid dripped onto the table in front of him.

"If things were different, I'd have given them a pass. Hell, I'd have joined them."

The screen flipped to another page. *Project Early Light, Special Pathogens Lab Access*, then a list of eight names. *Lang, Jennifer* was first, the second was *Barnes, John Joseph*.

"Project Early Light was a USAMRIID Black Box job, completely off the books."

"Lang led the vaccine team," said Gath.

Carter laughed, a disturbingly wet sound. "Jennifer Lang never made a vaccine in her life."

Another image appeared on the screen. An ID from Aegis Laboratories. *U.S. Army Combat Capabilities*

Development Command. Dr. Jennifer Lang, Head of Section,
Biological Agents, Weapons and Materials Research
Division.

"Lang led pathogen development. White's Disease was her baby and Barnes was on her team. In her bed too, left his wife for her. But look at me, getting all moral. Barnes gave a sample to the Faction. The original airborne strain was fast. While Barnes was safe on the station and Lang was underground at Aegis, the Faction released White's Disease in Frederick Towne Mall."

"John wouldn't kill innocent people."

"Have you looked outside? He killed everyone."

Carter wheezed and rubbed his red-rimmed eyes. They were already growing pale. He took the pink notebook from his pouch and laid it on the table, the metal vial resting on top.

"It's all in Lang's notebook. It's mostly research notes, but there's a diary too. I knew most of it already. The Faction were fanatics. This was their last chance to take their country back. They were soldiers, veterans, heroes. Who better to take over when the country was on its knees? But it spread too fast. By the time the government fell, there was nothing left."

Gath tried to make sense of it all.

"Then why did he give me a vaccine?"

"He didn't give you a vaccine, he gave you the disease. The original airborne strain. You brought it back for him. The Faction's still out there, special forces live for this kind of shit. Lexington was the only thing in their way. Now we're gone. We were infiltrated. They used one of the vials you brought back to take us off the board."

"You should have told me this on the station. I could have talked to John, you didn't have to kill him."

"I didn't kill him."

Gath stared at him. "You killed him because of the vials."

"I didn't even know about the vials. My orders were to keep him alive. He was our link to the others."

Gath's mind reeled. He slumped into the nearest chair.

"If you didn't kill him, who did?"

"I don't know. I was told not to trust anyone on the crew."

"Even me?"

"Especially you. You were his friend. He picked you."

Carter coughed wetly and spat out dark gobbets.

"Listen, I need a favor." He grinned showing blood-stained teeth. "I know the timing's not great, old buddy, but I don't have long. Sobek. I need you to find her."

"I don't care about Sobek."

"She was in contact with survivors, building a network. Only she knows where they are. If the Faction gets the locations, they'll strip them of everything they have. You have to find her."

"How can I get her back from guys like that? I can hardly stand up."

"You wouldn't be my first choice, old man, but my first choices are all dead. Look in Manhattan. Sobek said there was Faction activity in Manhattan. I didn't get details. It was pillow talk, didn't want to spoil the mood."

Gath shook his head. "You want me to search Manhattan for your girlfriend?"

"I'm a romantic." He shrugged. "I'd help if I could, old-timer."

He held out the notebook and vial. "Give these to Sobek when you find her. She'll know what to do. She always does."

Gath leaned across the table and took them. Carter touched a control and the door slid open.

"I'll let Maria out when you're close."

Gath stood and looked at the man who used to be his friend.

"No last words," said Carter. "Just go."

It didn't take long for Gath to find Remikov. Nozzles appeared in the walls and they were sprayed with chemical decontamination as the elevator arrived. Gath didn't say much, only that Carter was dead and it was over. That was enough. There was too much bubbling inside him to make any sense. Discarding the biohazard suits in the Oval, they made their way back to the entrance of the West Wing. The doors had blown open and they stared into a blizzard. Snow fell heavily, whipped into waves by the wind.

"Can't see a damned thing," said Gath. "Bikes'll be no use in this."

Remikov nodded. "We can wait."

Gath grabbed the doors to close them and looked up. Someone was out there, approaching through the storm. Remikov drew a pistol but Gath laid a hand on her arm. The figure was near enough to see the ragged remains of a uniform, a scarf around its head. One arm was missing.

"Who is it?" asked the Russian, raising her voice against the wind.

"A friend," said Gath.

He pushed the doors wider and Walker strode passed him, coming in out of the cold.

Author's Note

Thank you for reading 'The Ragged Man', Book 2 in the 'On Nothing Hangs The Earth' series. If you liked the book, please consider leaving a review on Amazon. Book 1, 'On Nothing Hangs The Earth', is also available in eBook, hard copy, and audiobook format on Amazon and Audible.

Copyright © 2023 Tom Kline

Printed in Great Britain
by Amazon

21200276R00161